I've got that one, Reddie. And that one. And that one.

You sure have a lot of hats, Archie!

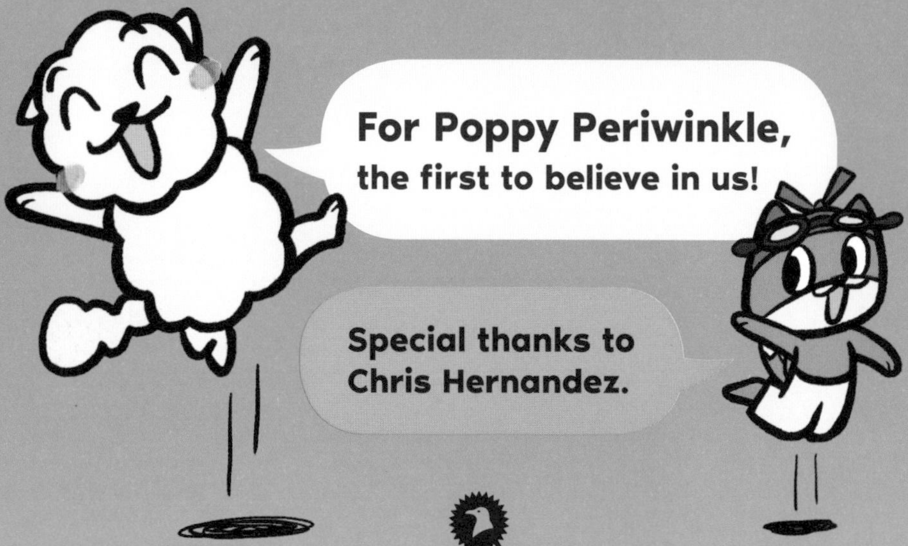
For Poppy Periwinkle,
the first to believe in us!
Special thanks to
Chris Hernandez.

RAZORBILL

An imprint of Penguin Random House LLC, New York

First published in the United States of America by Razorbill, an imprint of Penguin Random House LLC, 2021

Visit us online at penguinrandomhouse.com.

Library of Congress Cataloging-in-Publication Data
Names: Robertson, Nicholas James, author. | Robertson, Candy, illustrator.
Title: We will find your hat! : a conundrum / pictures and words by Candy James.
Description: New York : Razorbill, 2021. | Series: An Archie & Reddie book ; [2] | Audience: Ages 4-8 |
Summary: Fox cousins Archie and Reddie are back, and their mission is to find Archie's favorite hat, which has mysteriously gone missing, so they can enjoy the Hat Day party with all their friends.
Identifiers: LCCN 2021001338 | ISBN 9780593350133 (hardcover) | ISBN 9780593350140 (ebook) |
ISBN 9780593350157 (ebook) Subjects: LCSH: Graphic novels. | CYAC: Graphic novels. | Hats—Fiction. |
Lost and found possessions—Fiction. | Foxes—Fiction. | Cousins—Fiction. | Humorous stories.
Classification: LCC PZ7.7.R6325 We 2021 | DDC 741.5952—dc23
LC record available at https://lccn.loc.gov/2021001338

Manufactured in China

1 3 5 7 9 10 8 6 4 2

Book design by Candy James. Text set in Noir Pro.

A FREDDIE BOOK

WE WILL FIND YOUR HAT!

A CONUNDRUM!

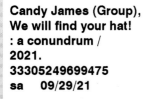

PICTURES AND WORDS BY

CANDY JAMES

RAZORBILL

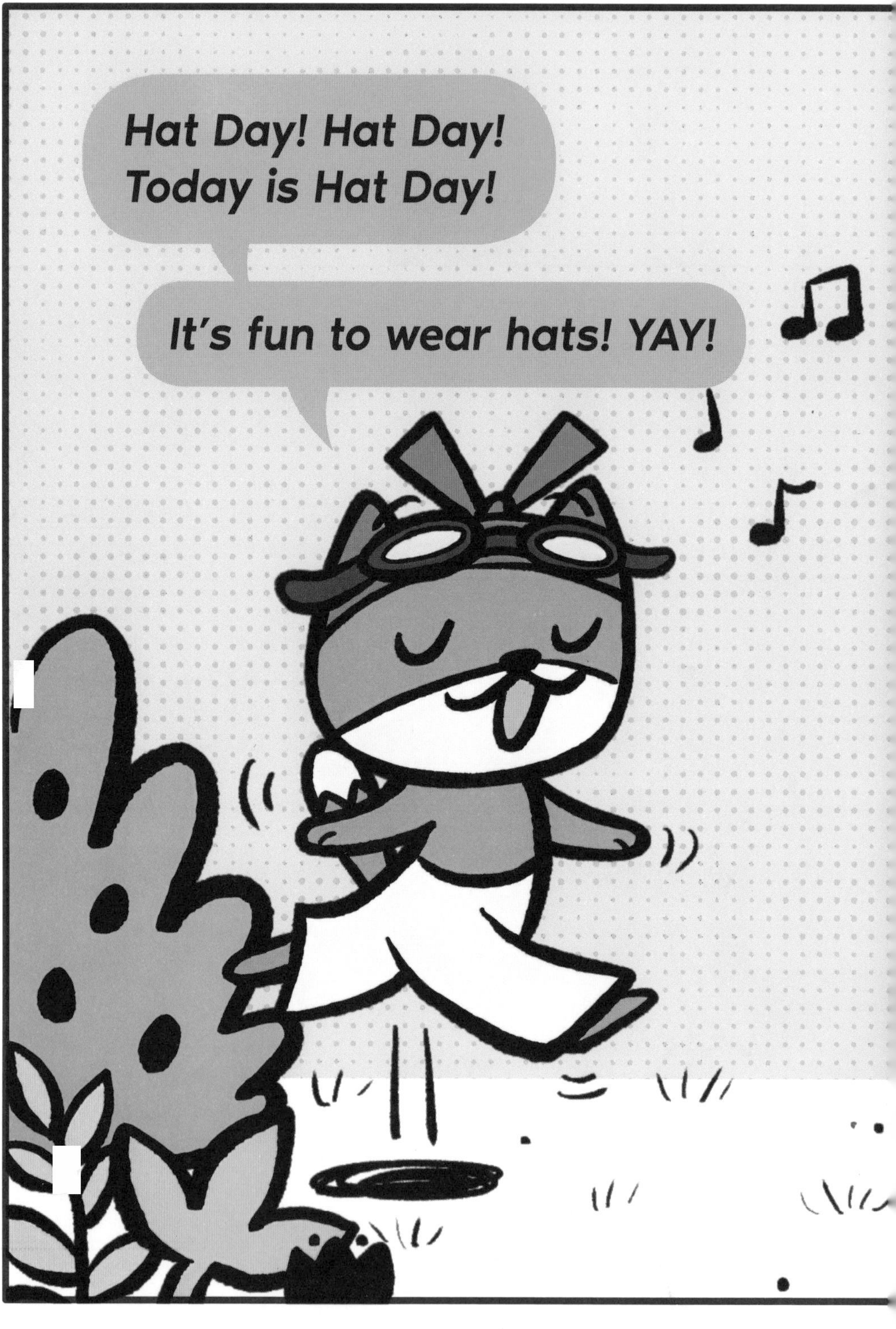
Hat Day! Hat Day!
Today is Hat Day!
It's fun to wear hats! YAY!

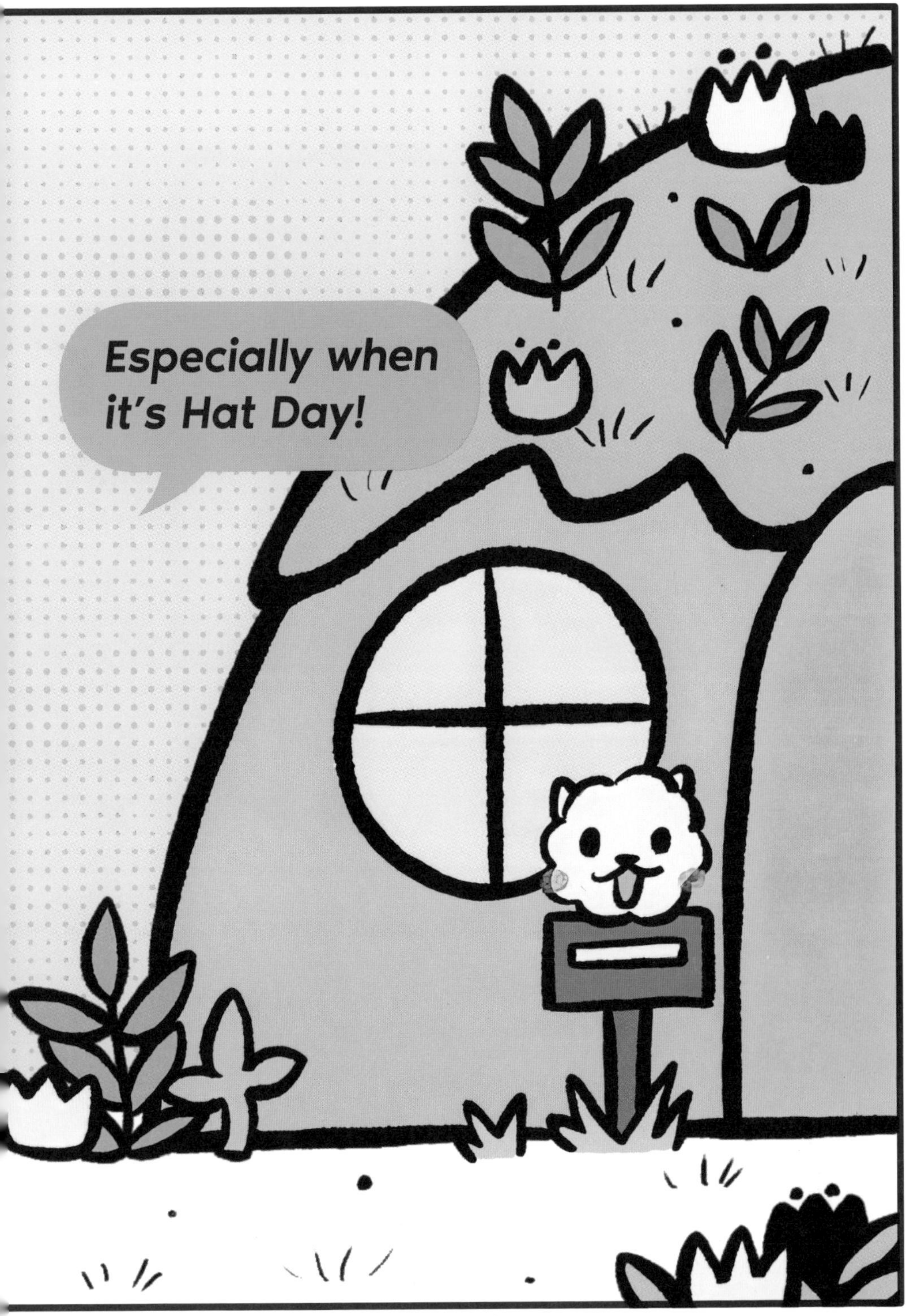
Especially when it's Hat Day!

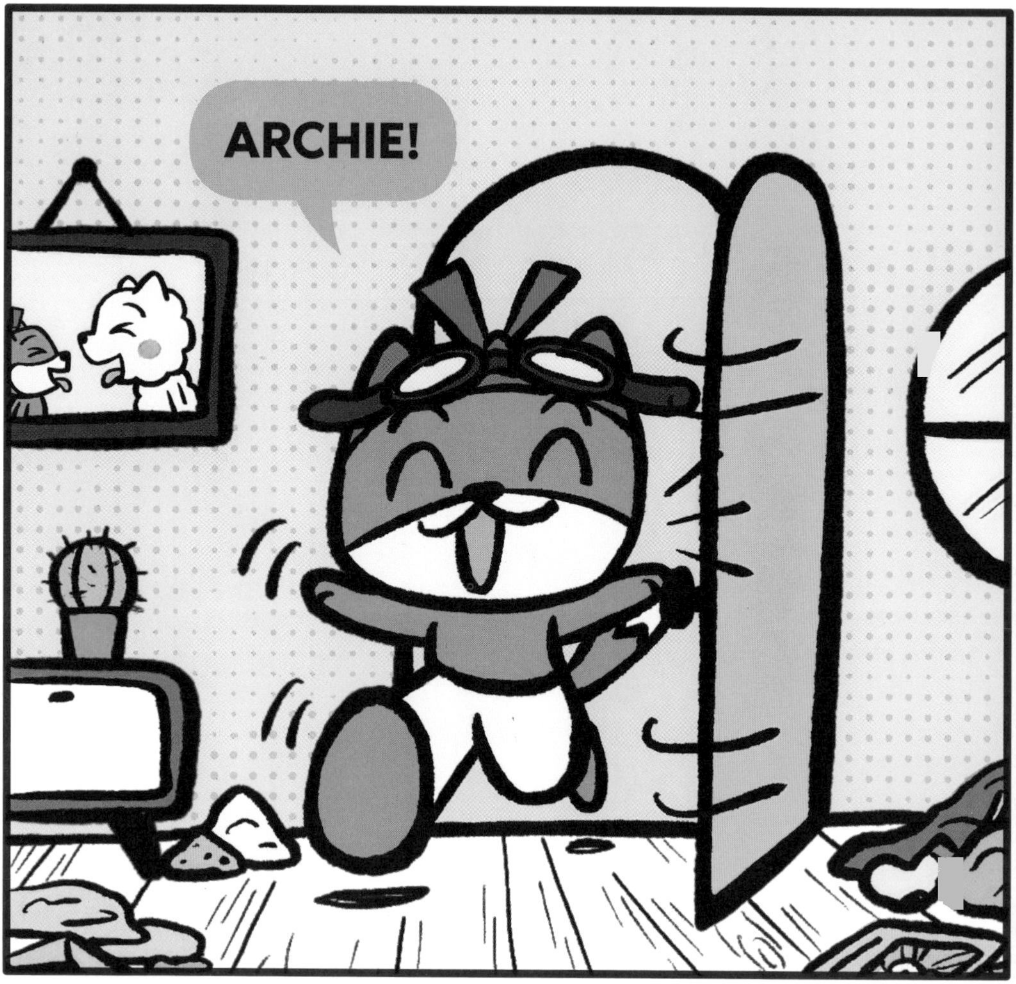
ARCHIE!

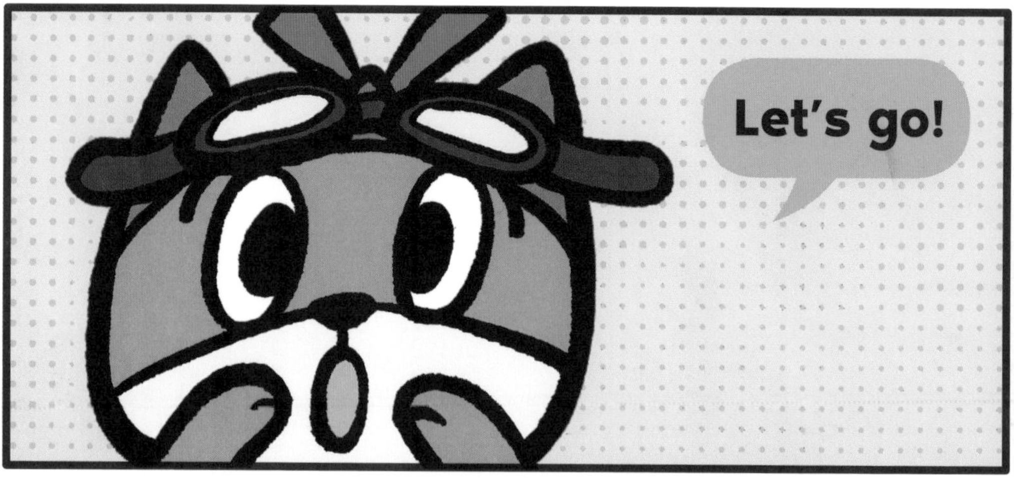
Let's go!

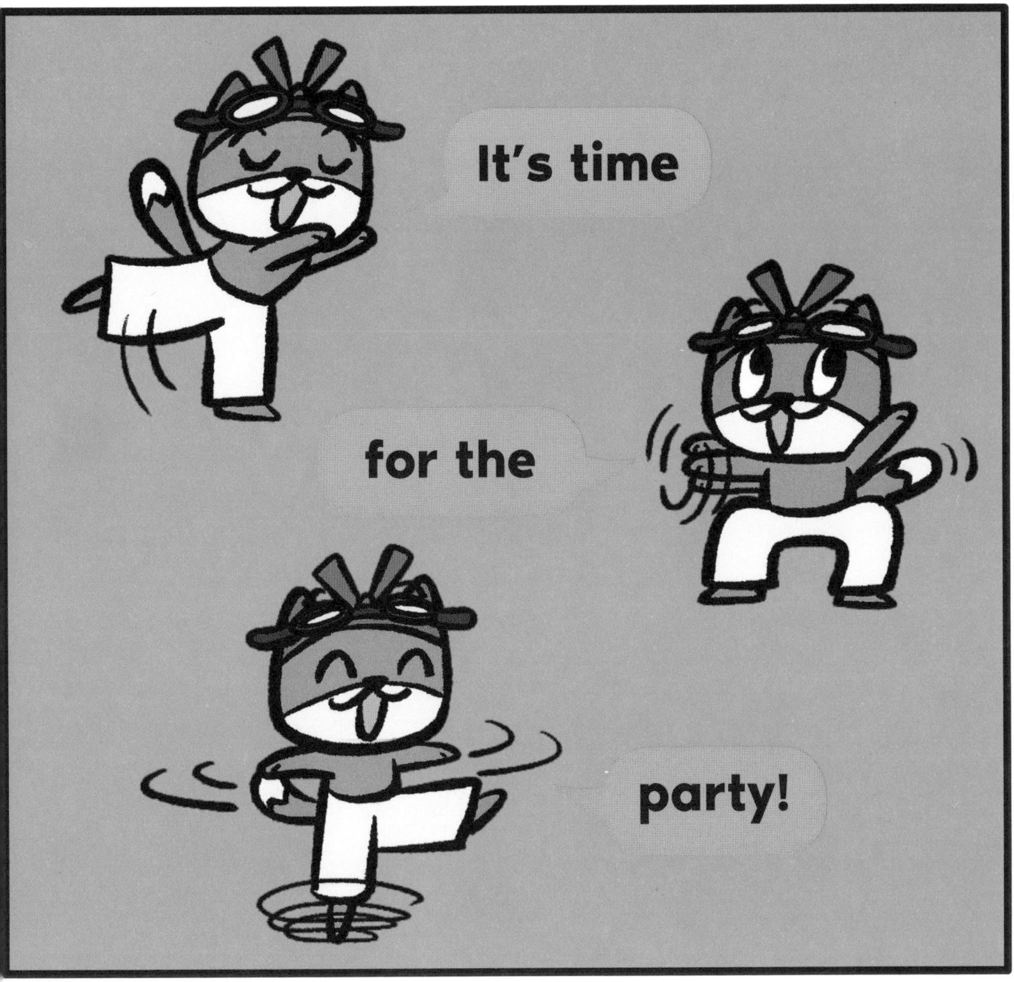
It's time
for the
party!

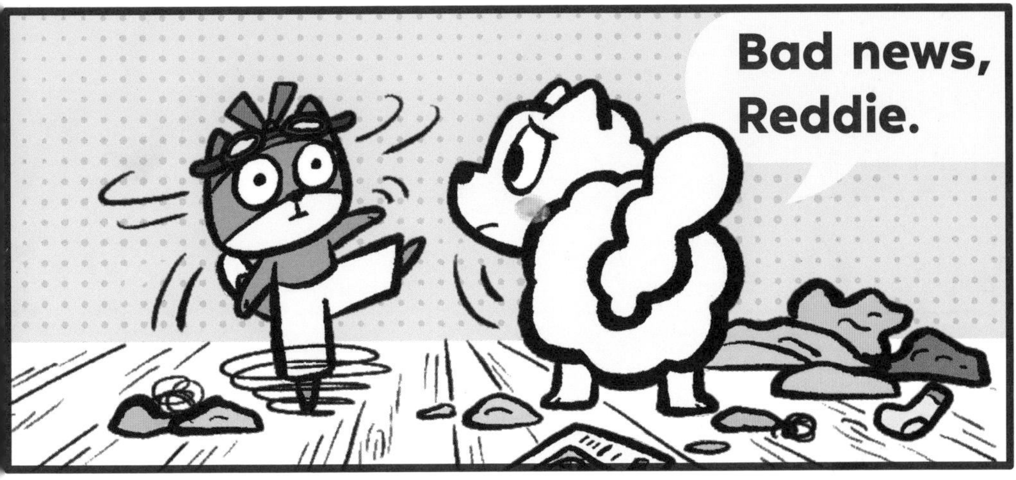
Bad news, Reddie.

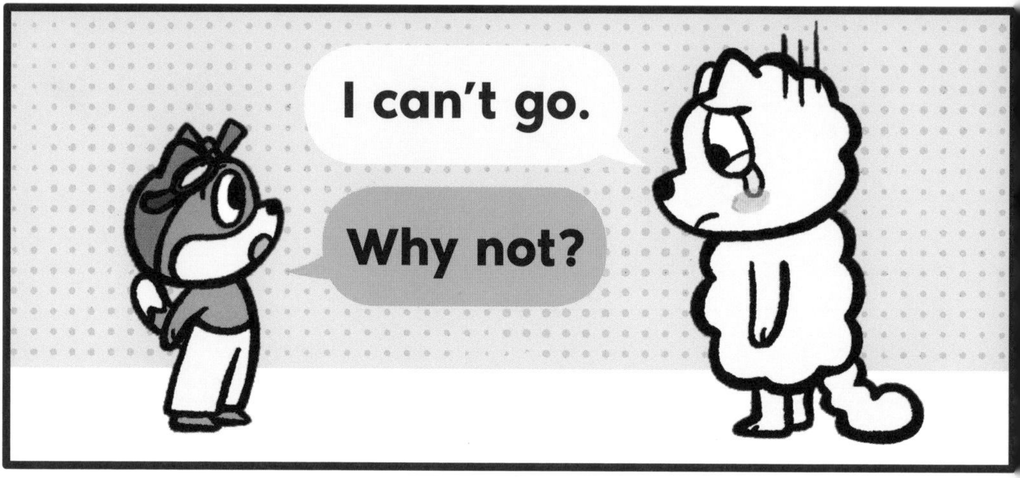
I can't go.
Why not?

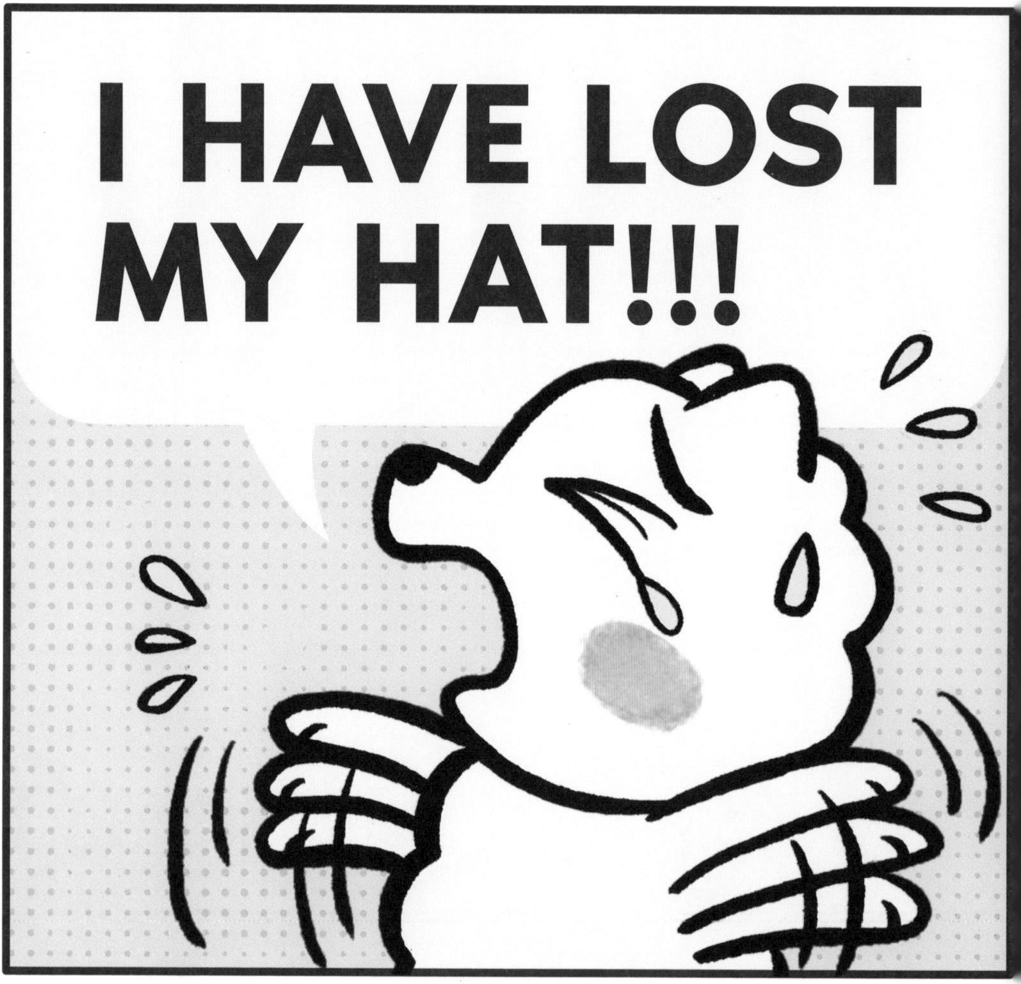
I HAVE LOST MY HAT!!!

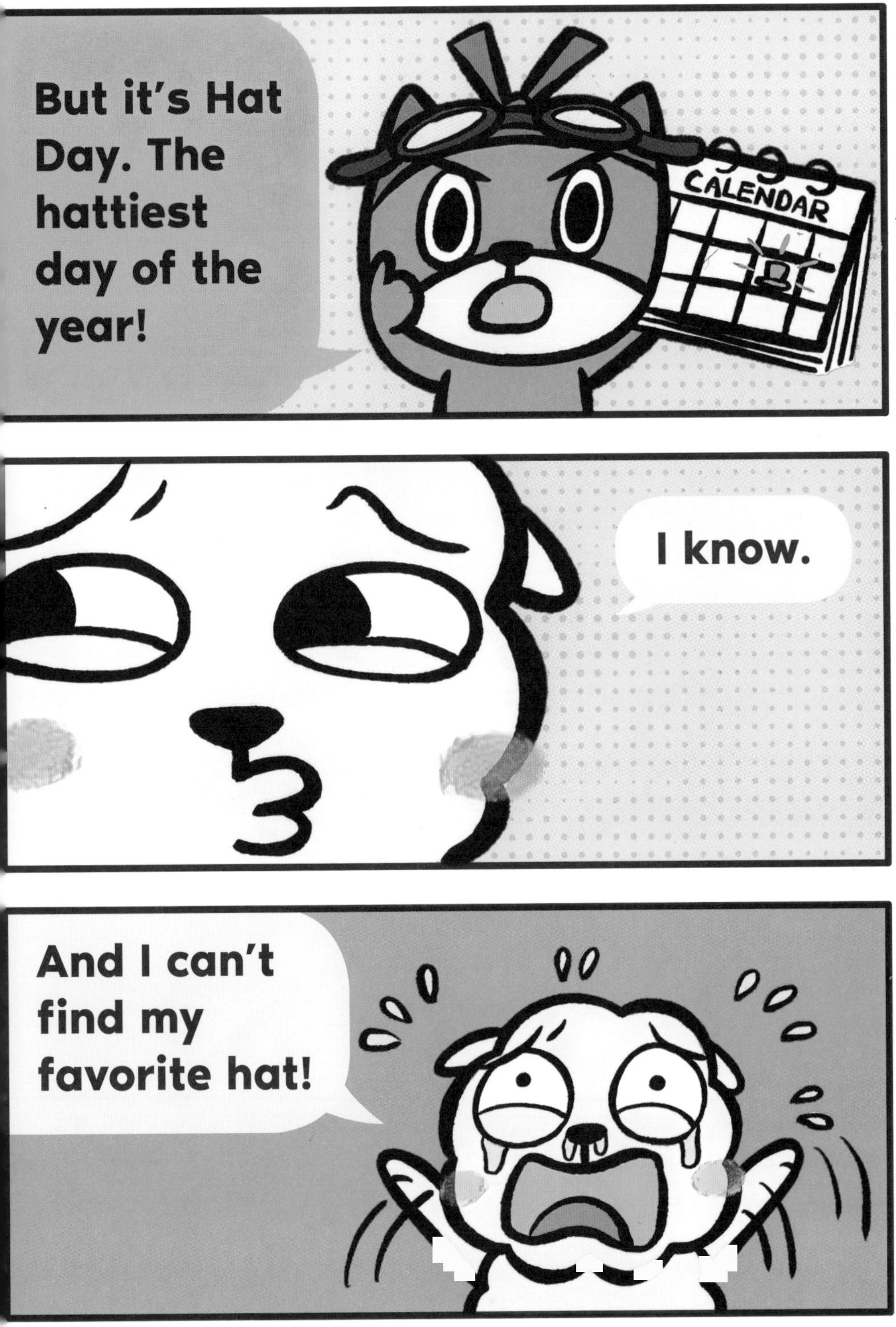
But it's Hat Day. The hattiest day of the year!
CALENDAR
I know.
And I can't find my favorite hat!

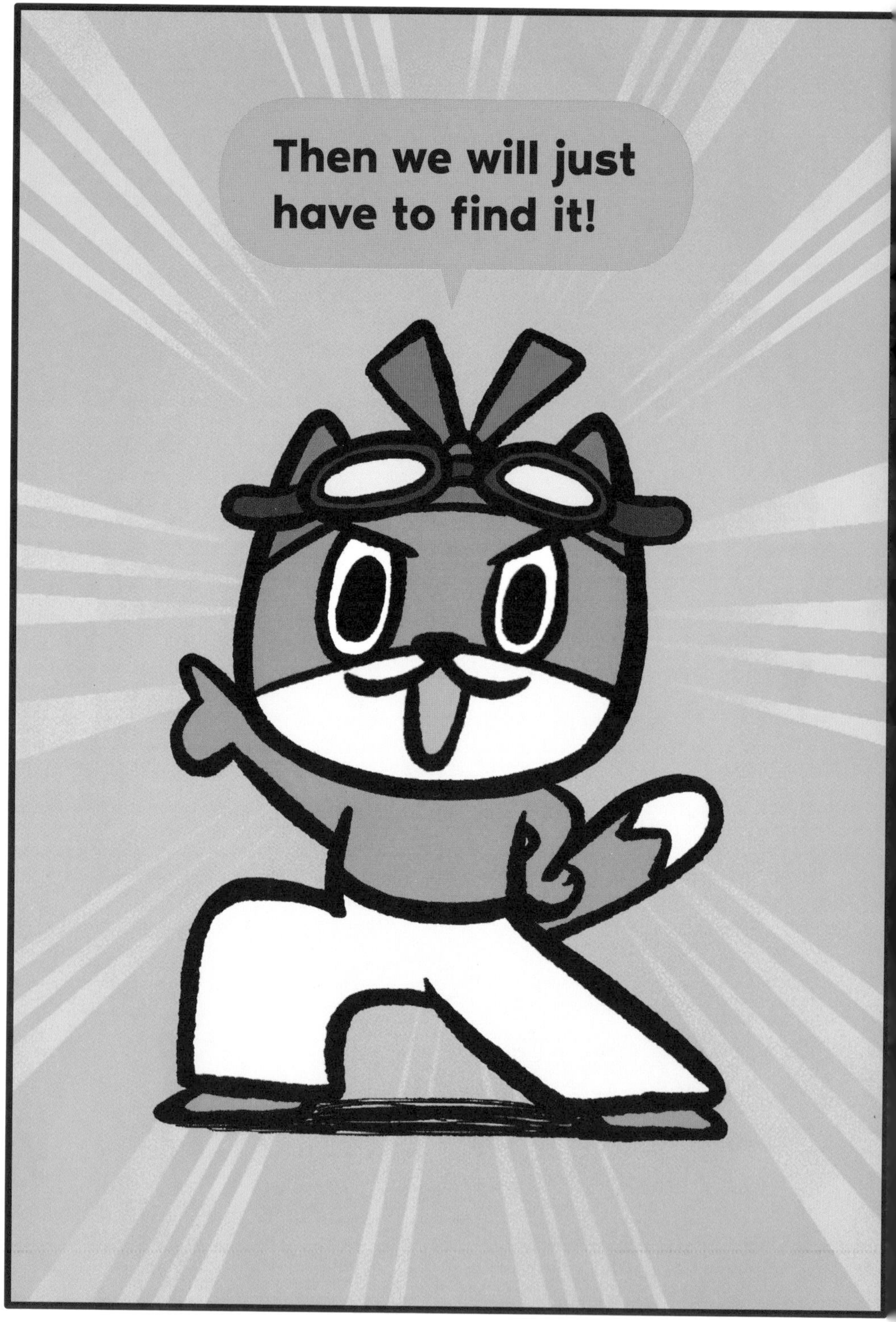
Then we will just have to find it!

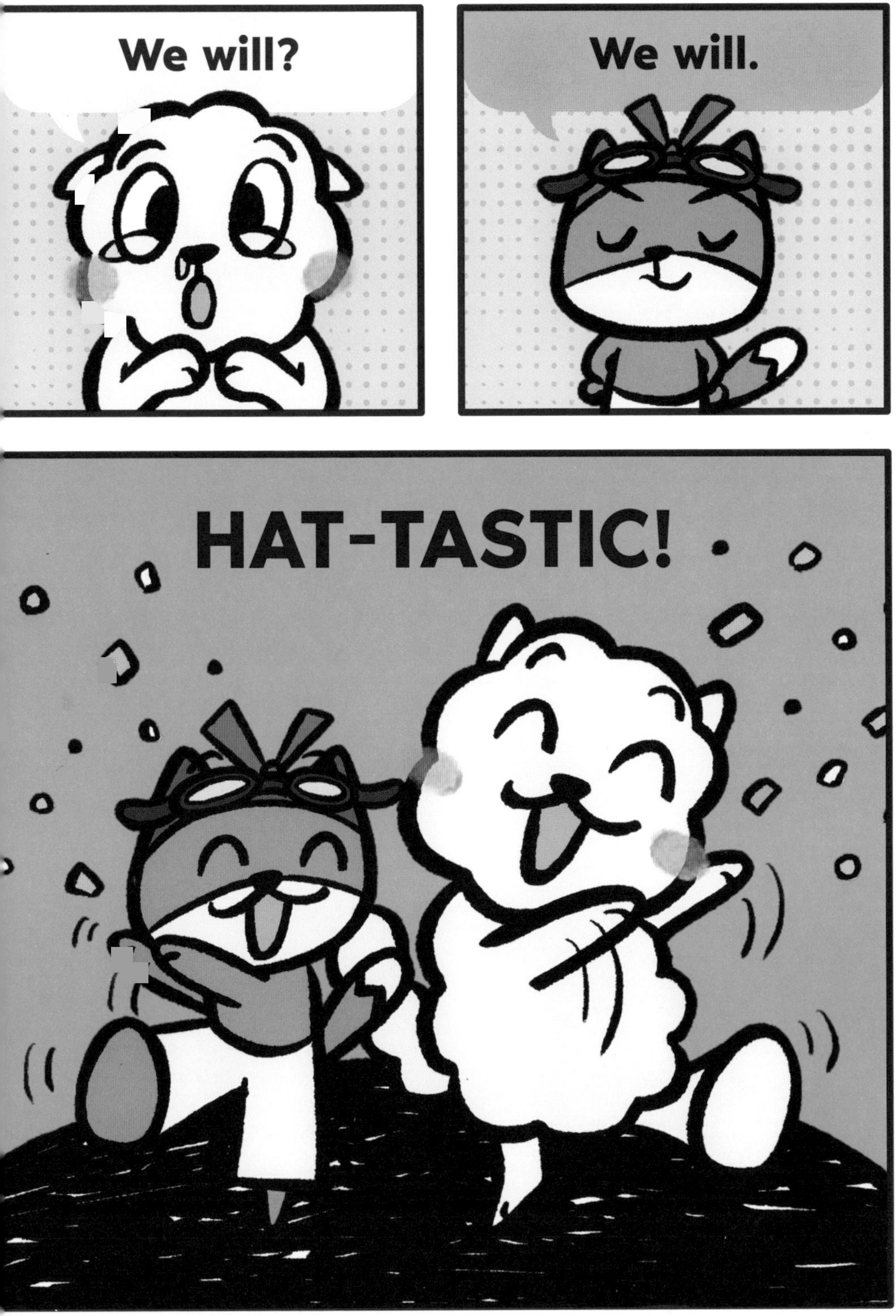
We will?
We will.
HAT-TASTIC!

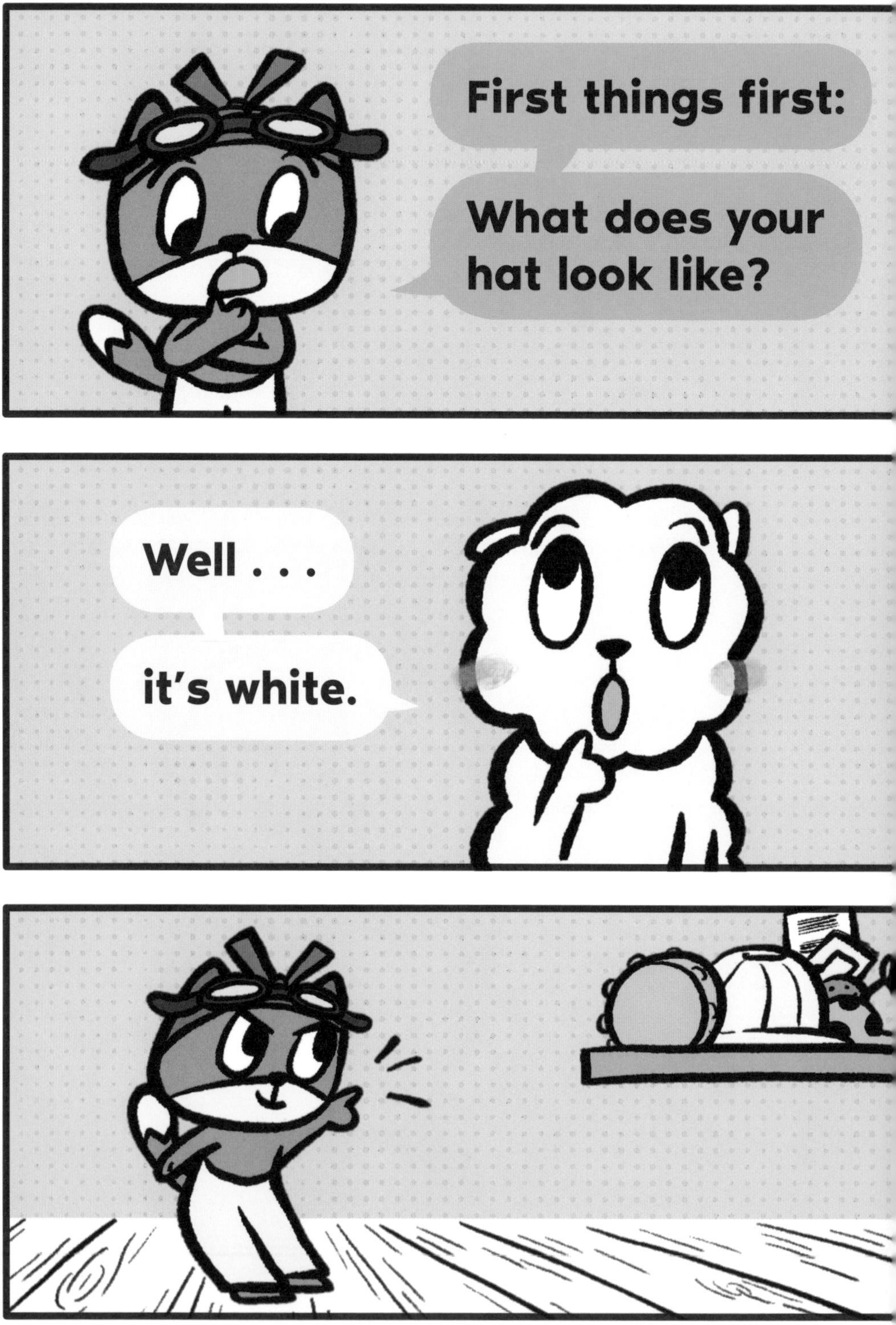
First things first:
What does your hat look like?
Well . . .
it's white.

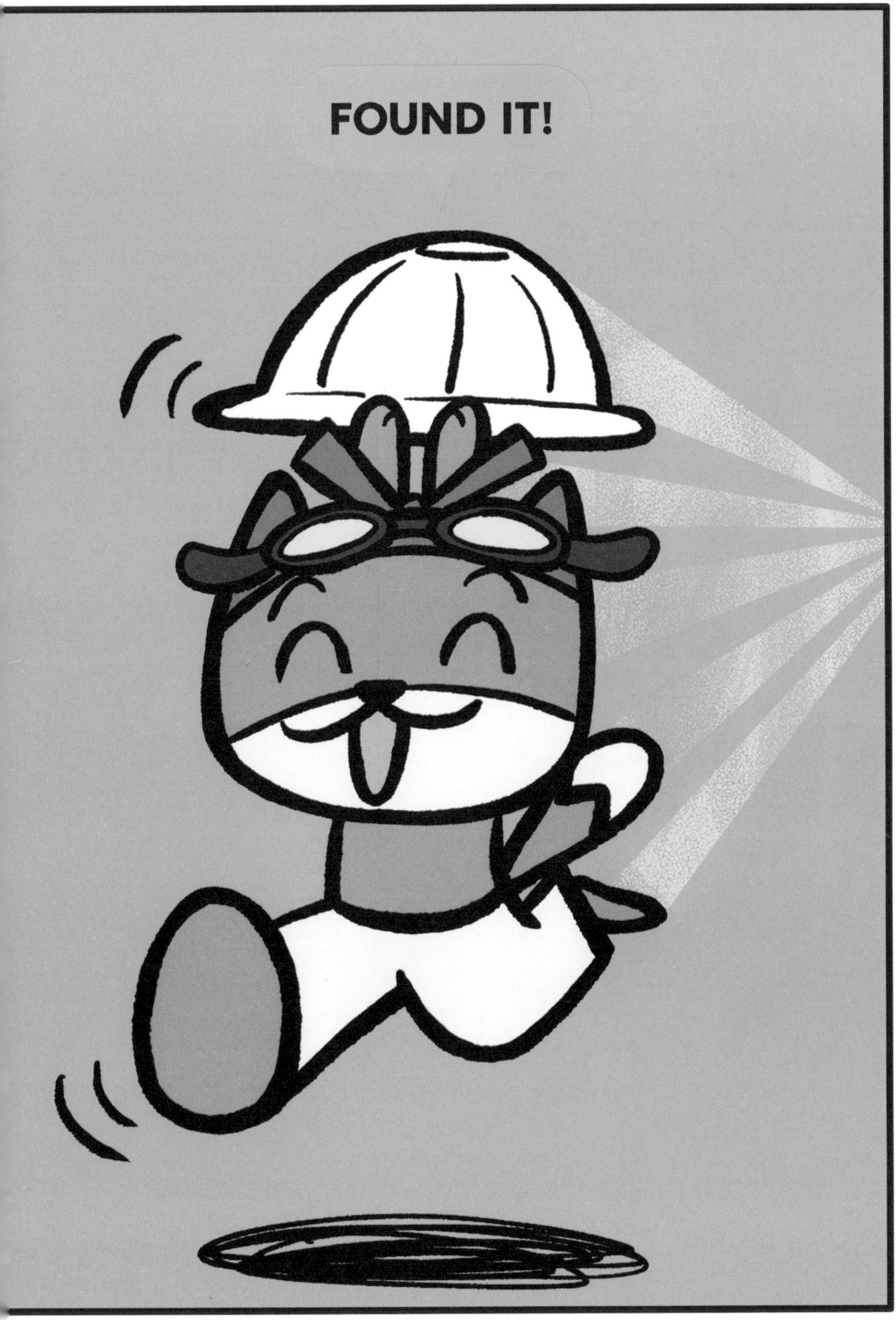
FOUND IT!

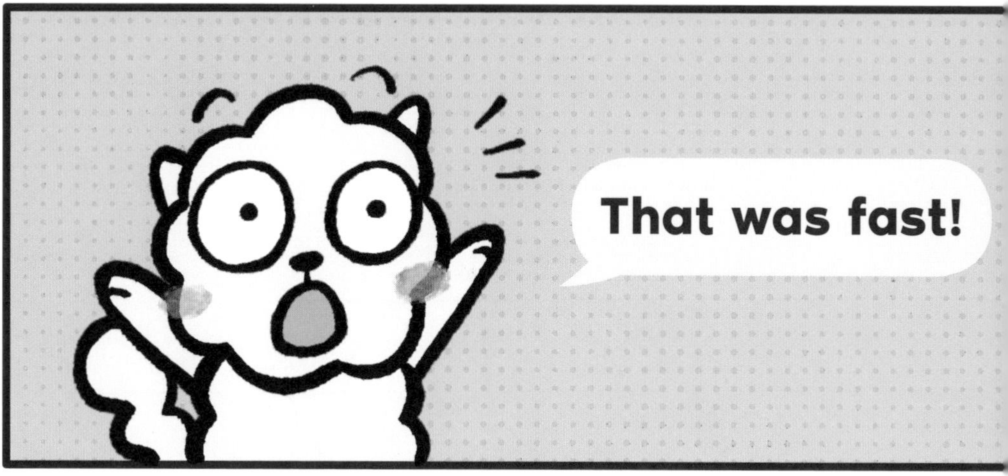
That was fast!

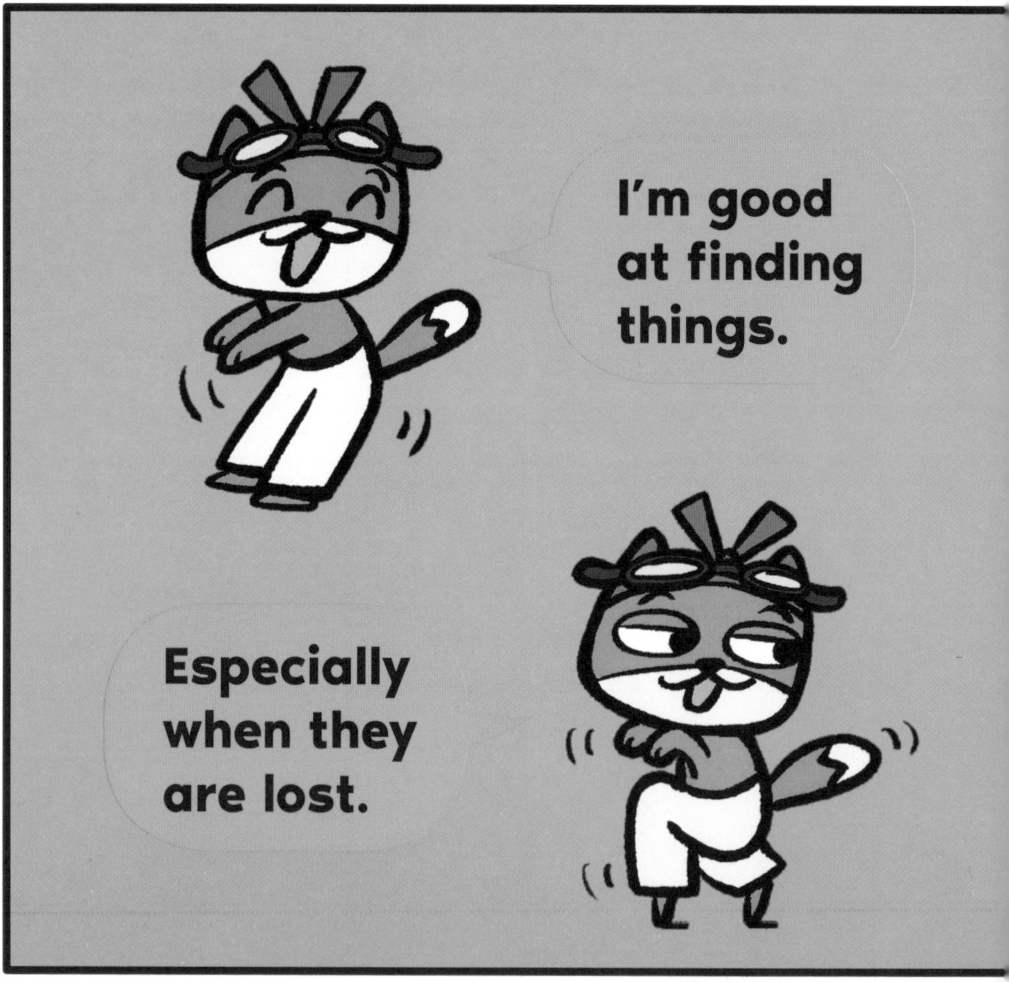
I'm good at finding things.
Especially when they are lost.

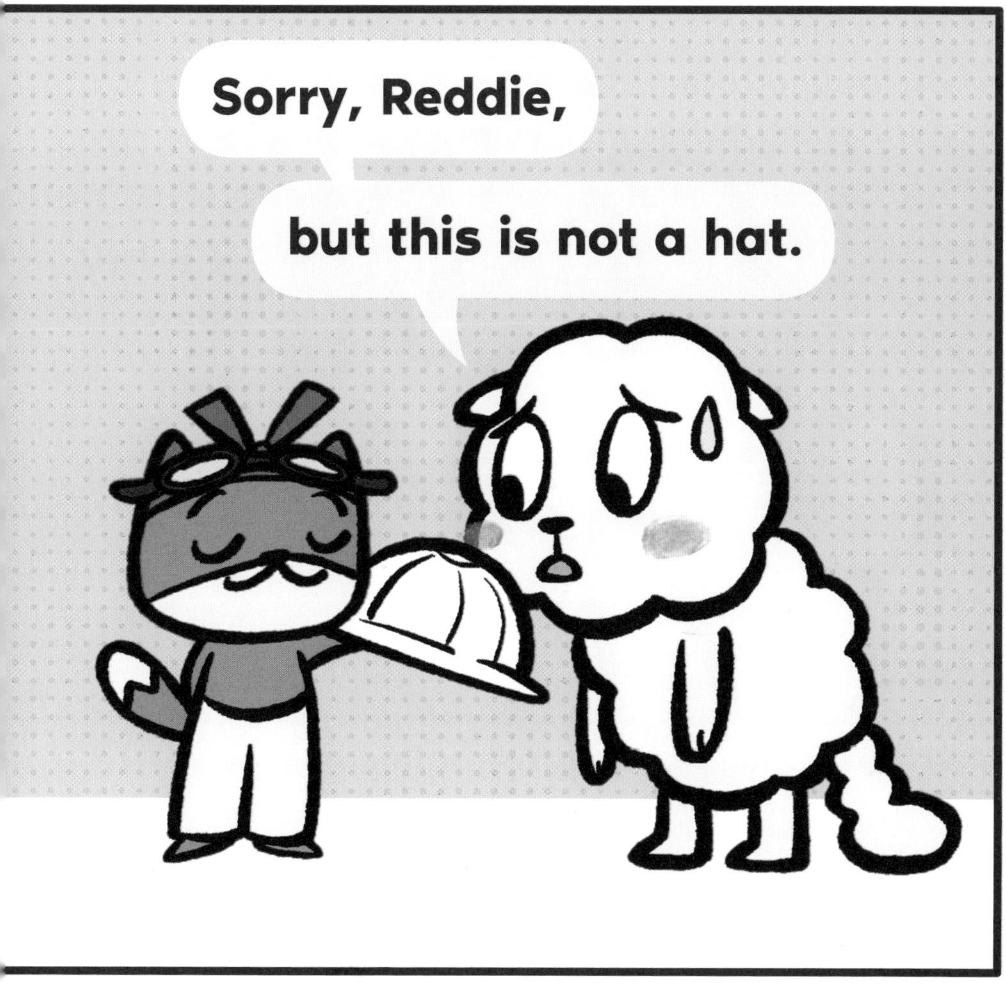
Sorry, Reddie,
but this is not a hat.

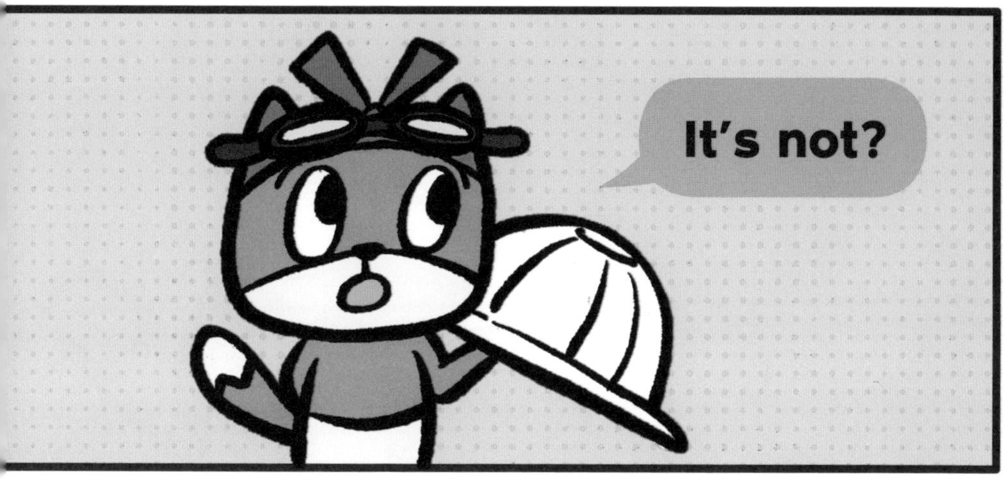
It's not?

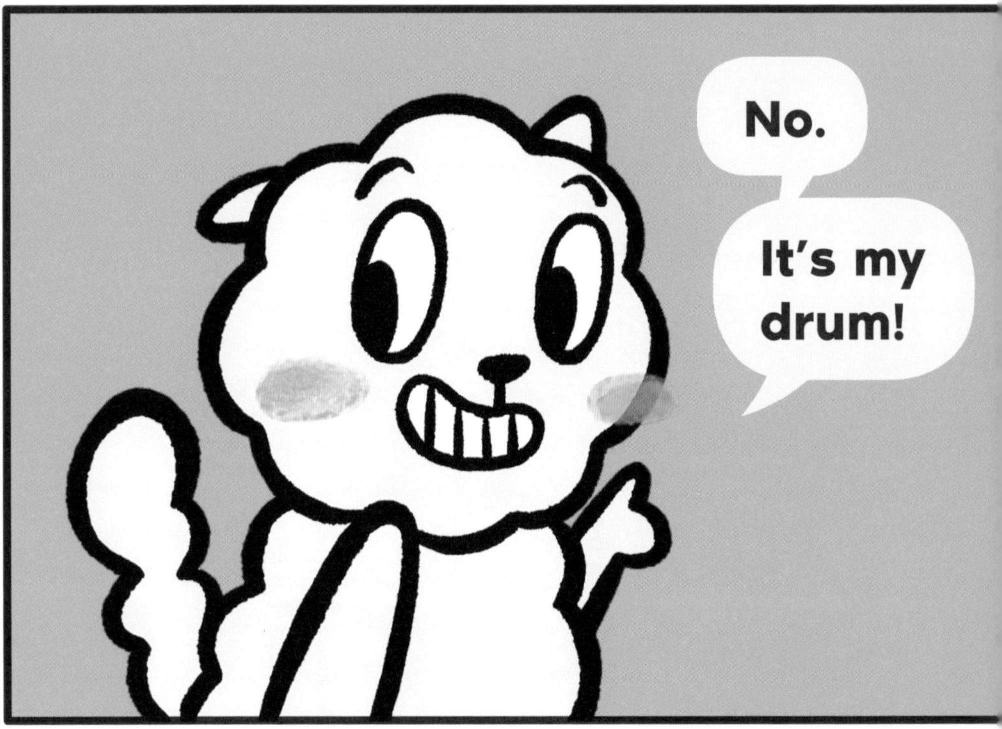
No.
It's my drum!
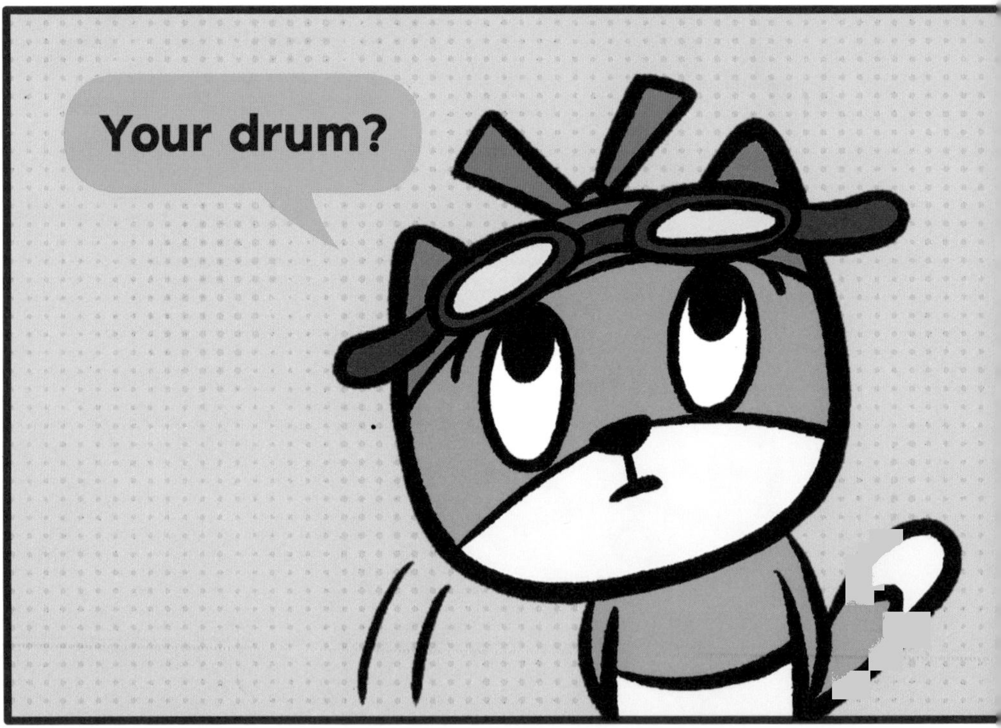
Your drum?

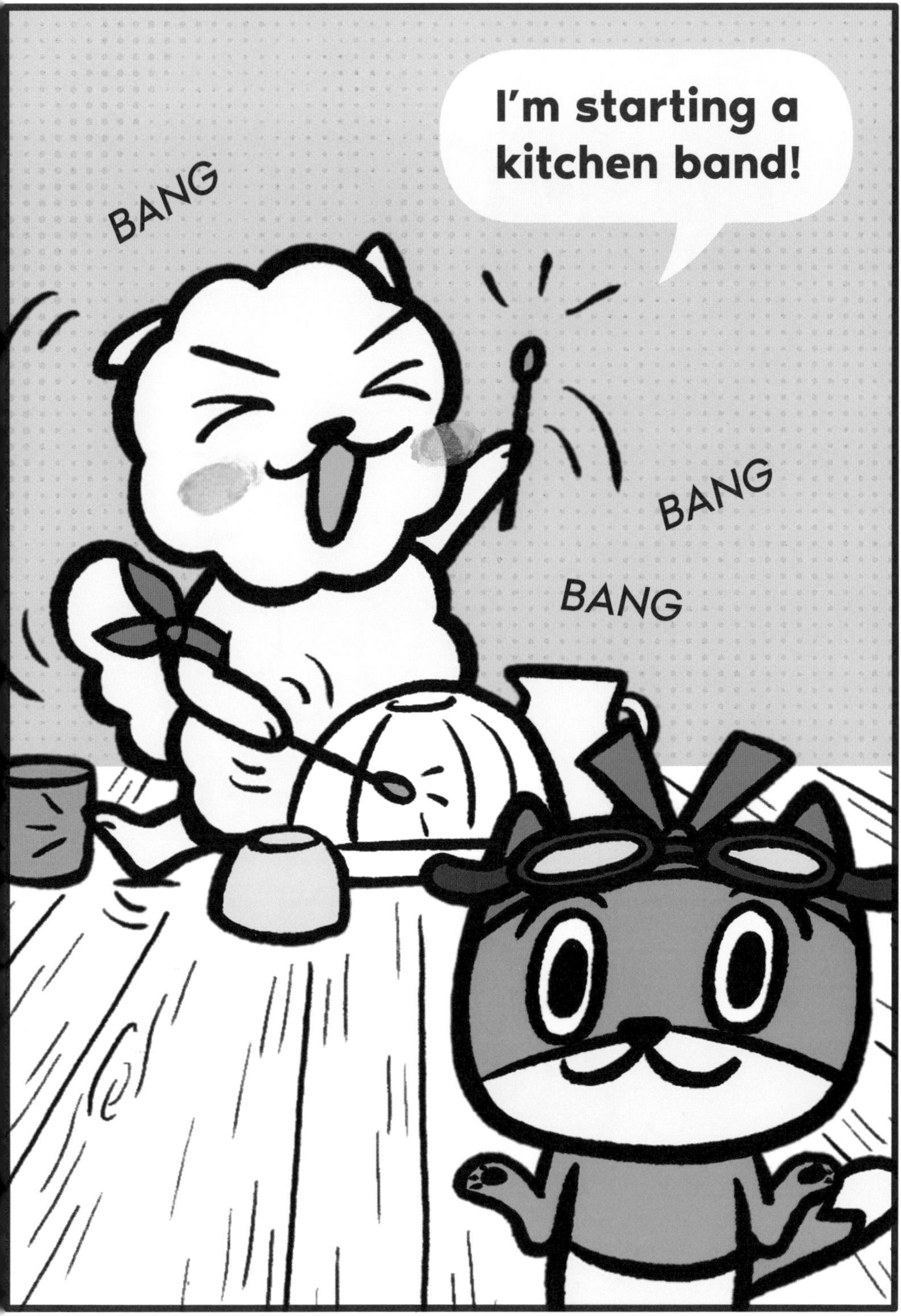
I'm starting a kitchen band!
BANG
BANG
BANG

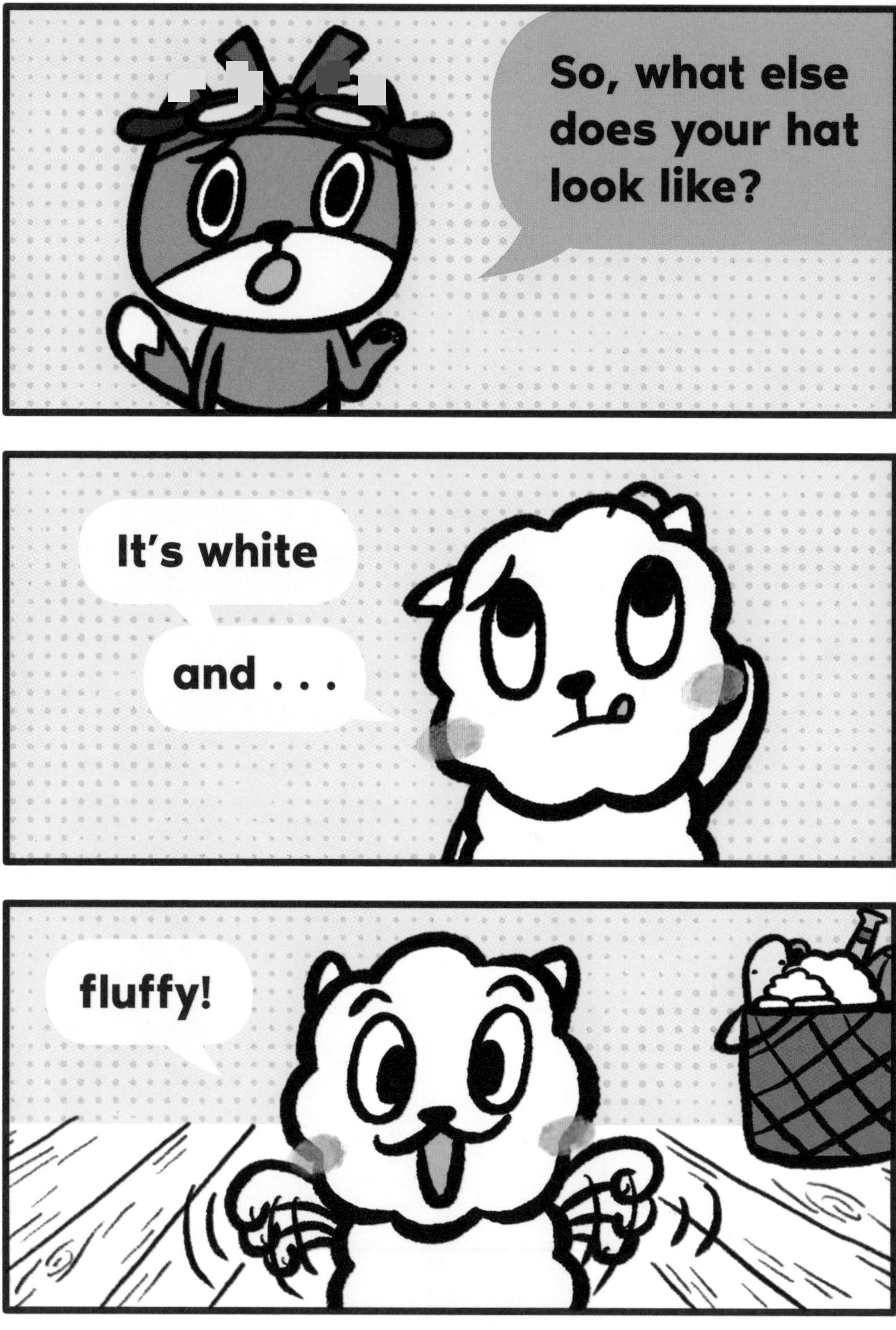
So, what else does your hat look like?
It's white
and . . .
fluffy!

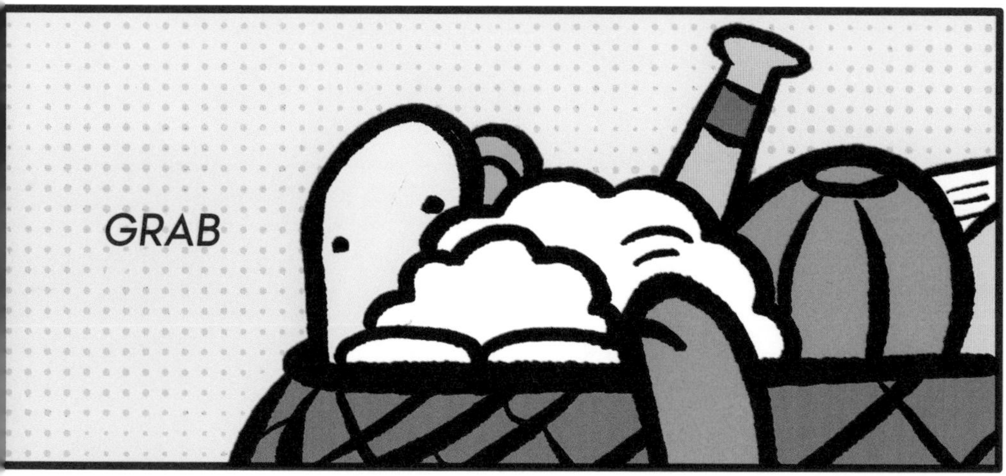
GRAB

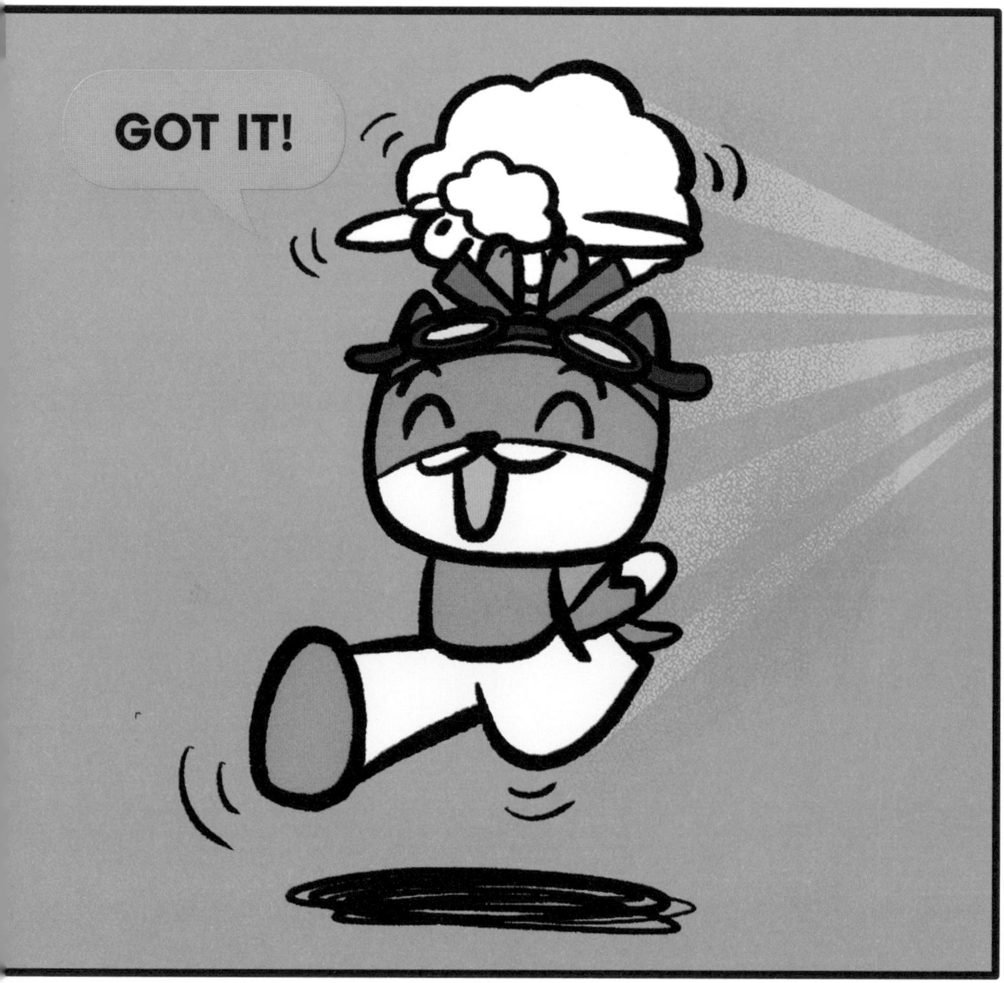
GOT IT!

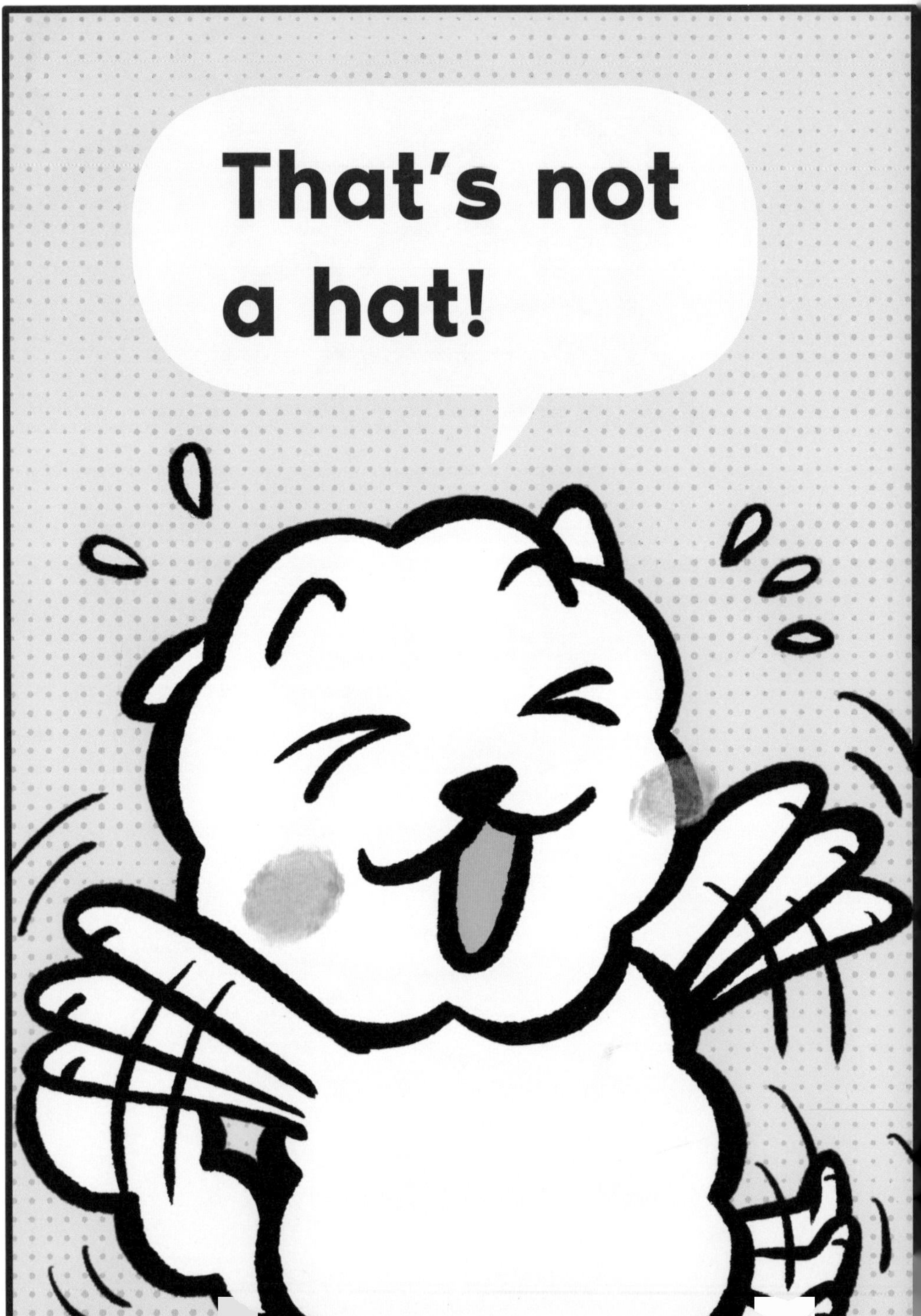
That's not a hat!

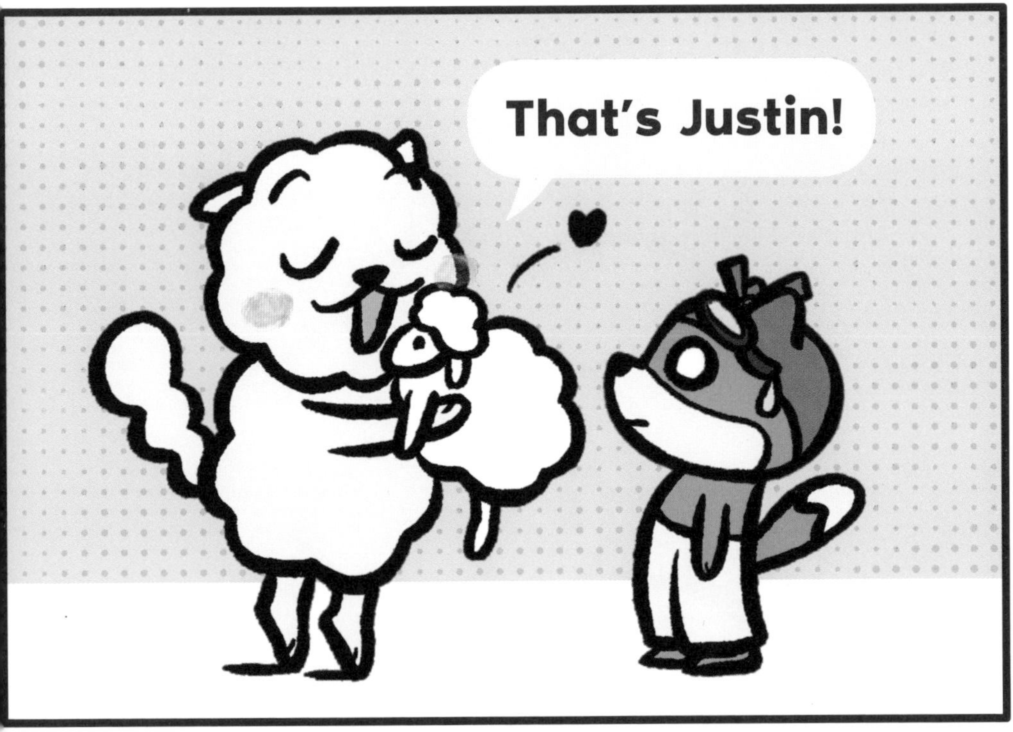
That's Justin!

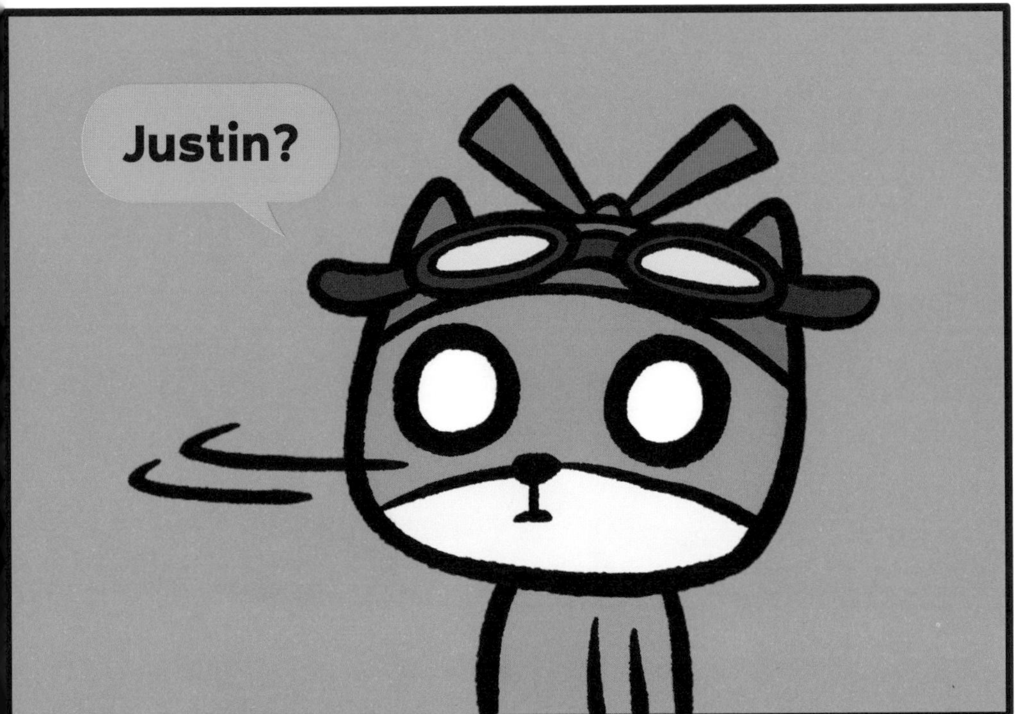
Justin?

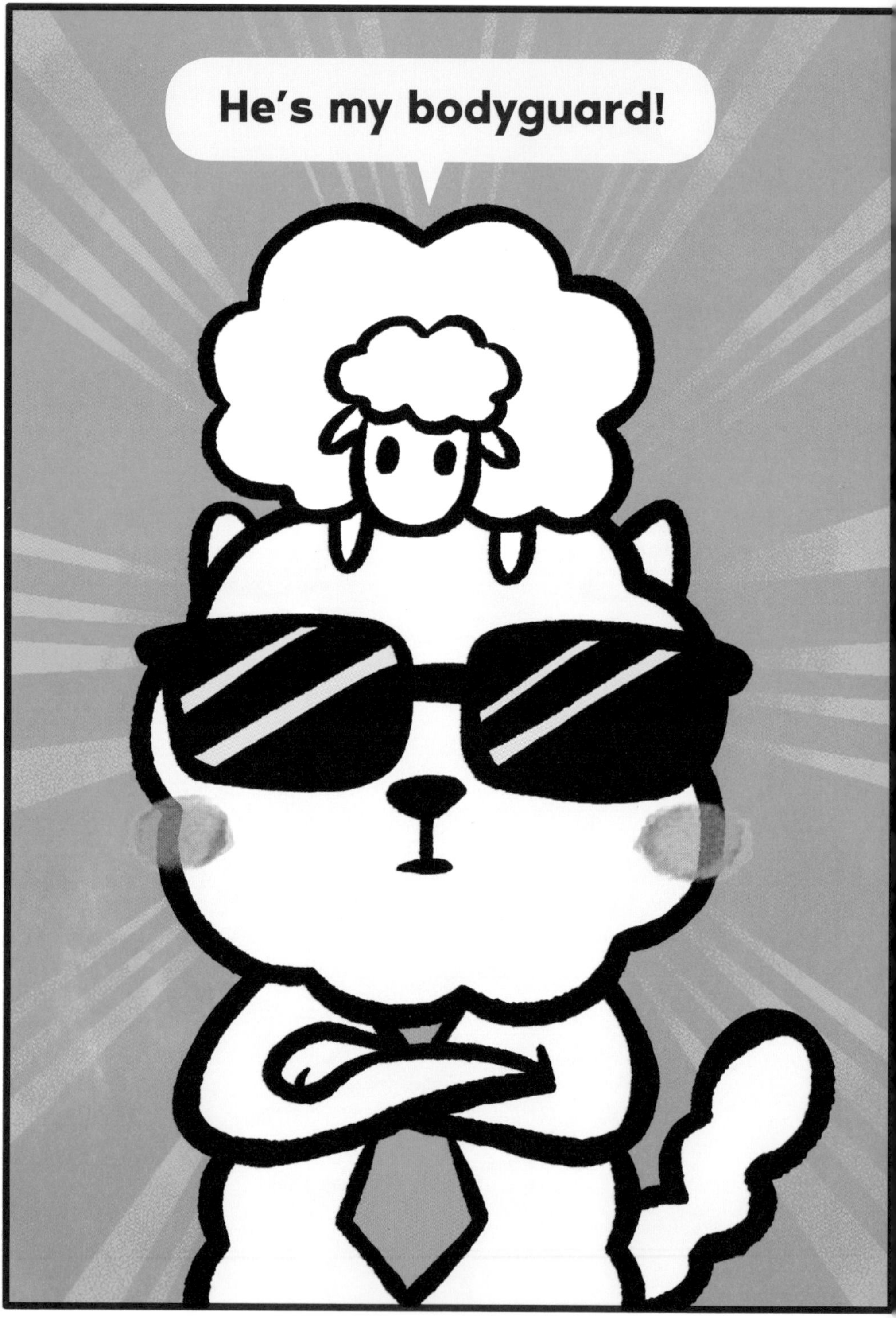
He's my bodyguard!

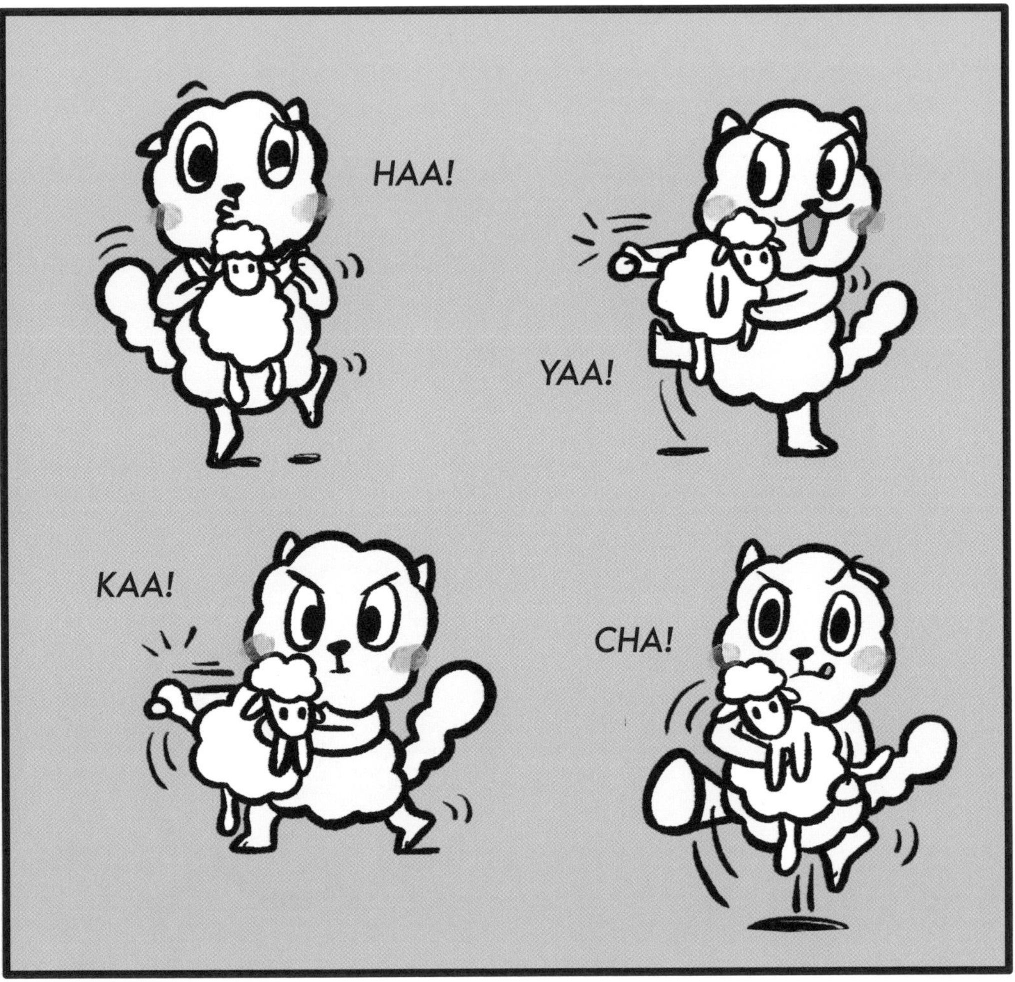
HAA!
YAA!
KAA!
CHA!

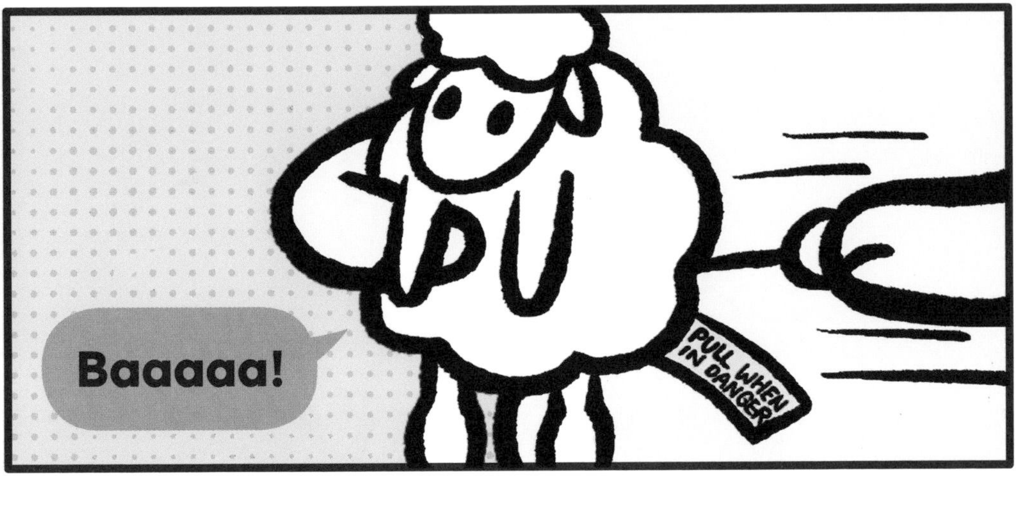
Baaaaa!
PULL WHEN
IN DANGER!

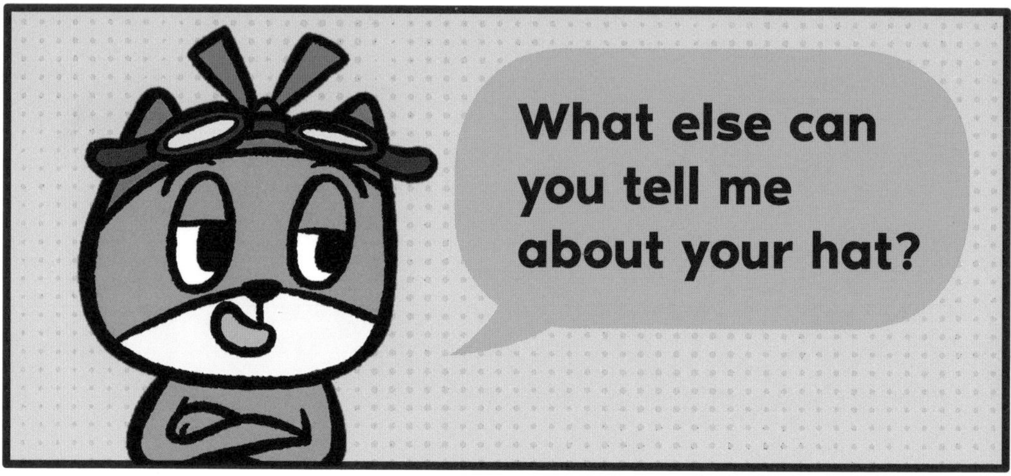
What else can you tell me about your hat?
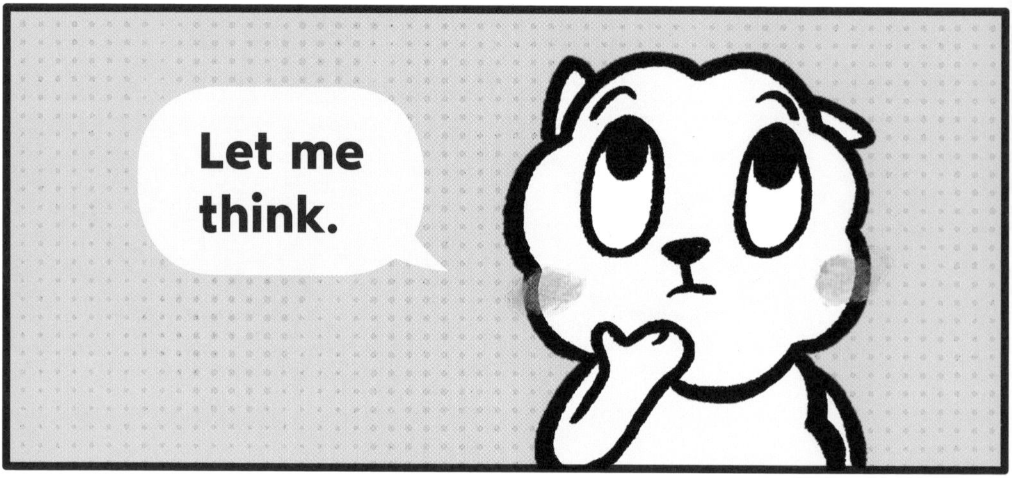
Let me think.
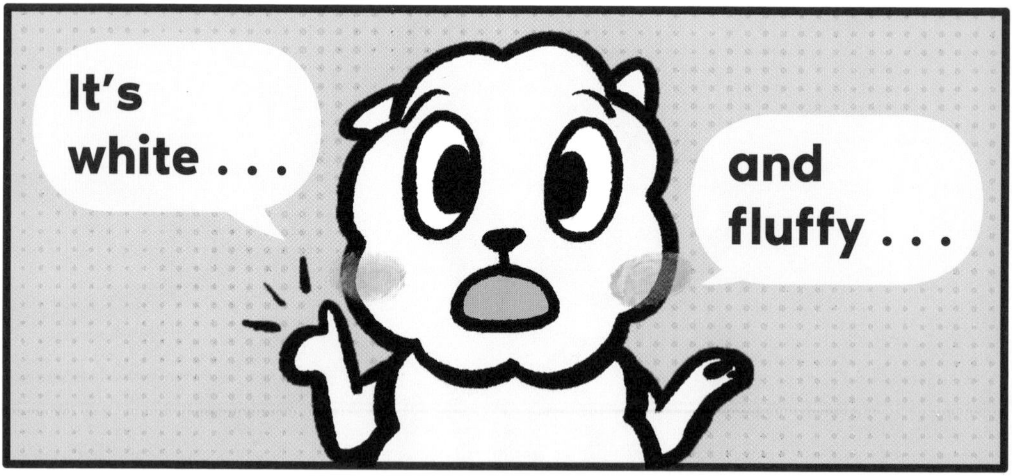
It's white . . .
and fluffy . . .

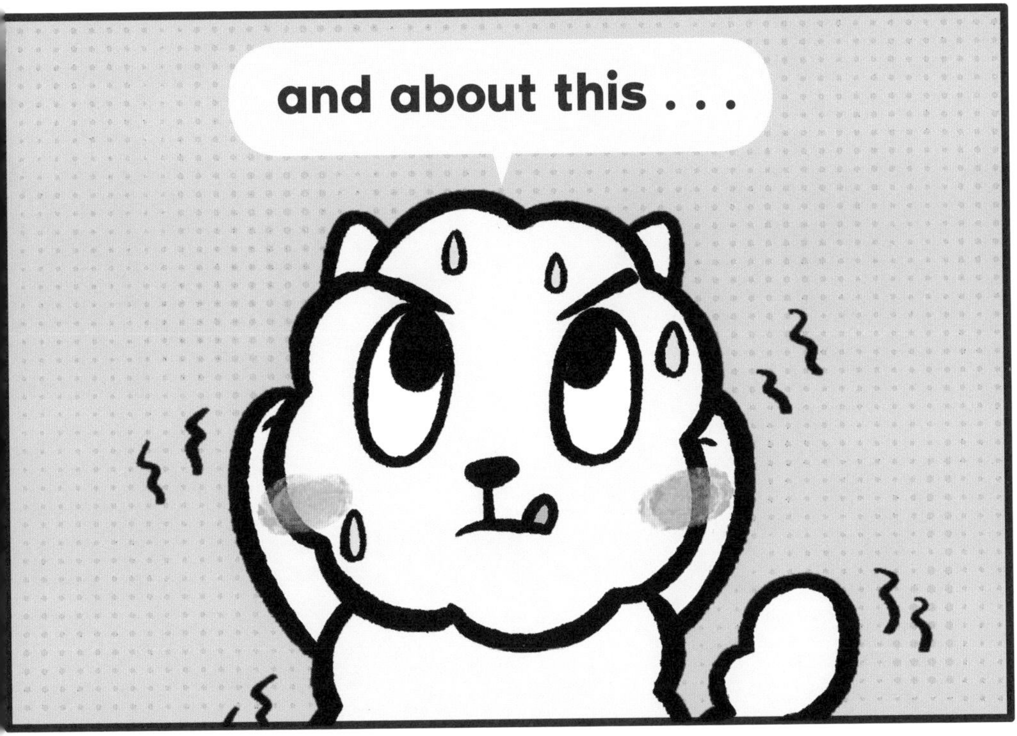
and about this . . .

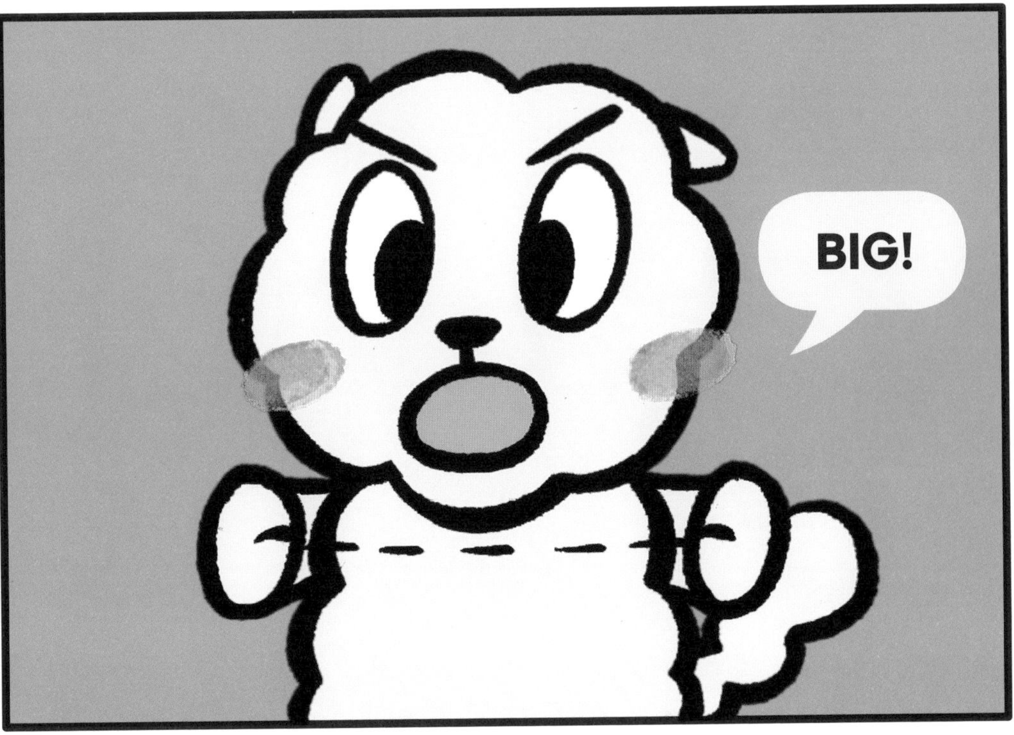
BIG!

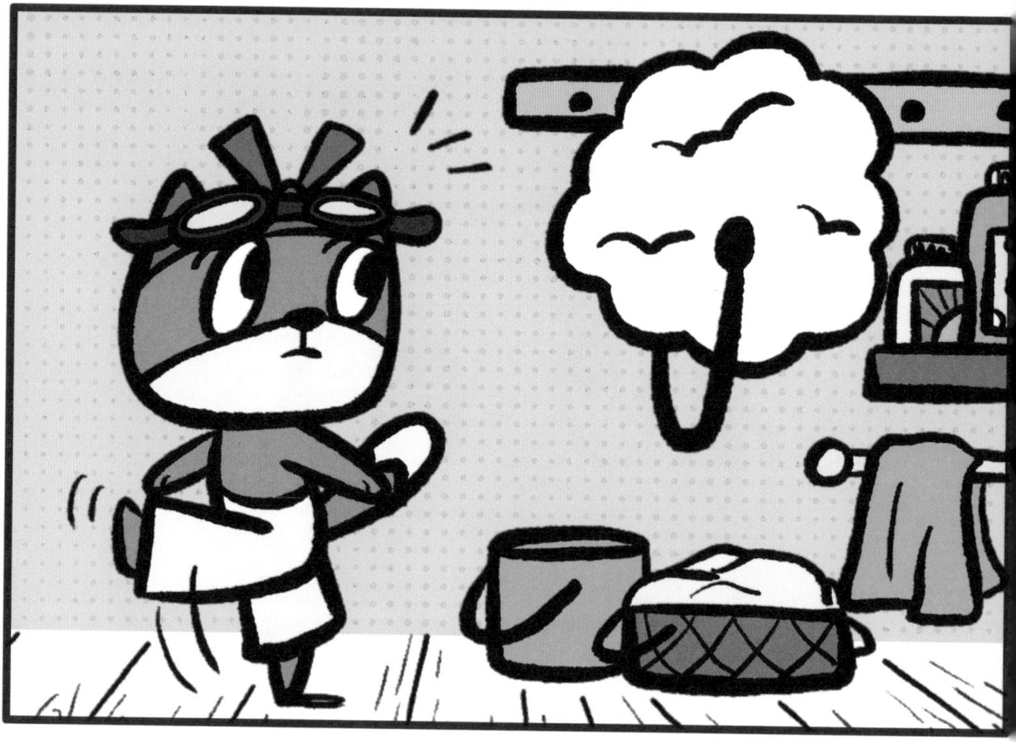

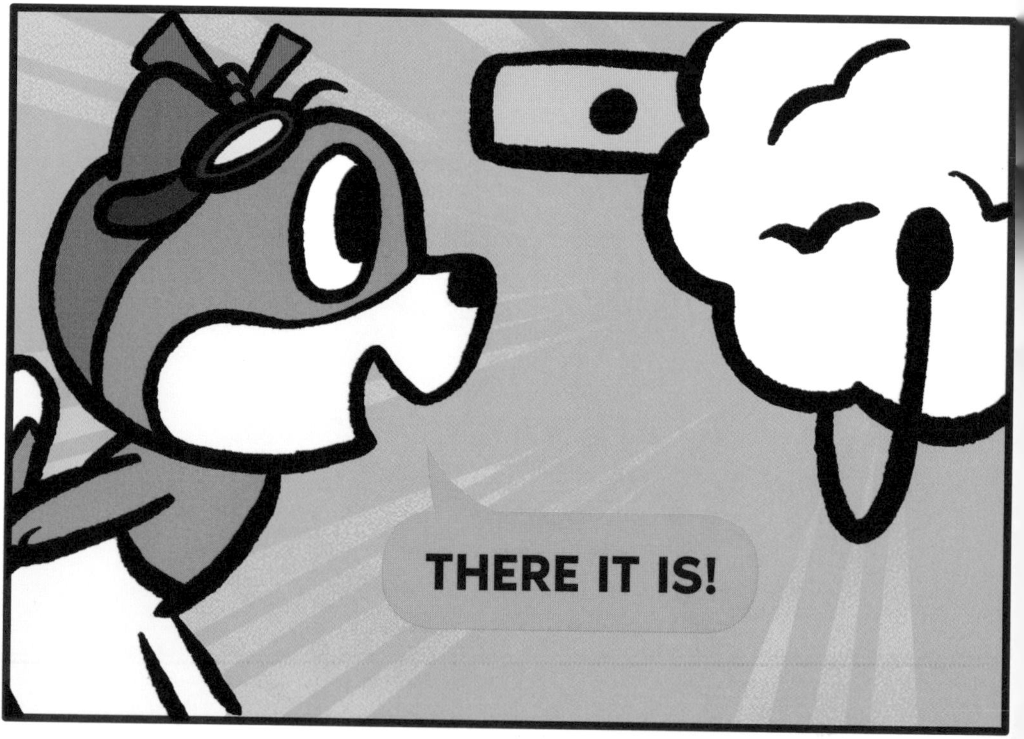
THERE IT IS!

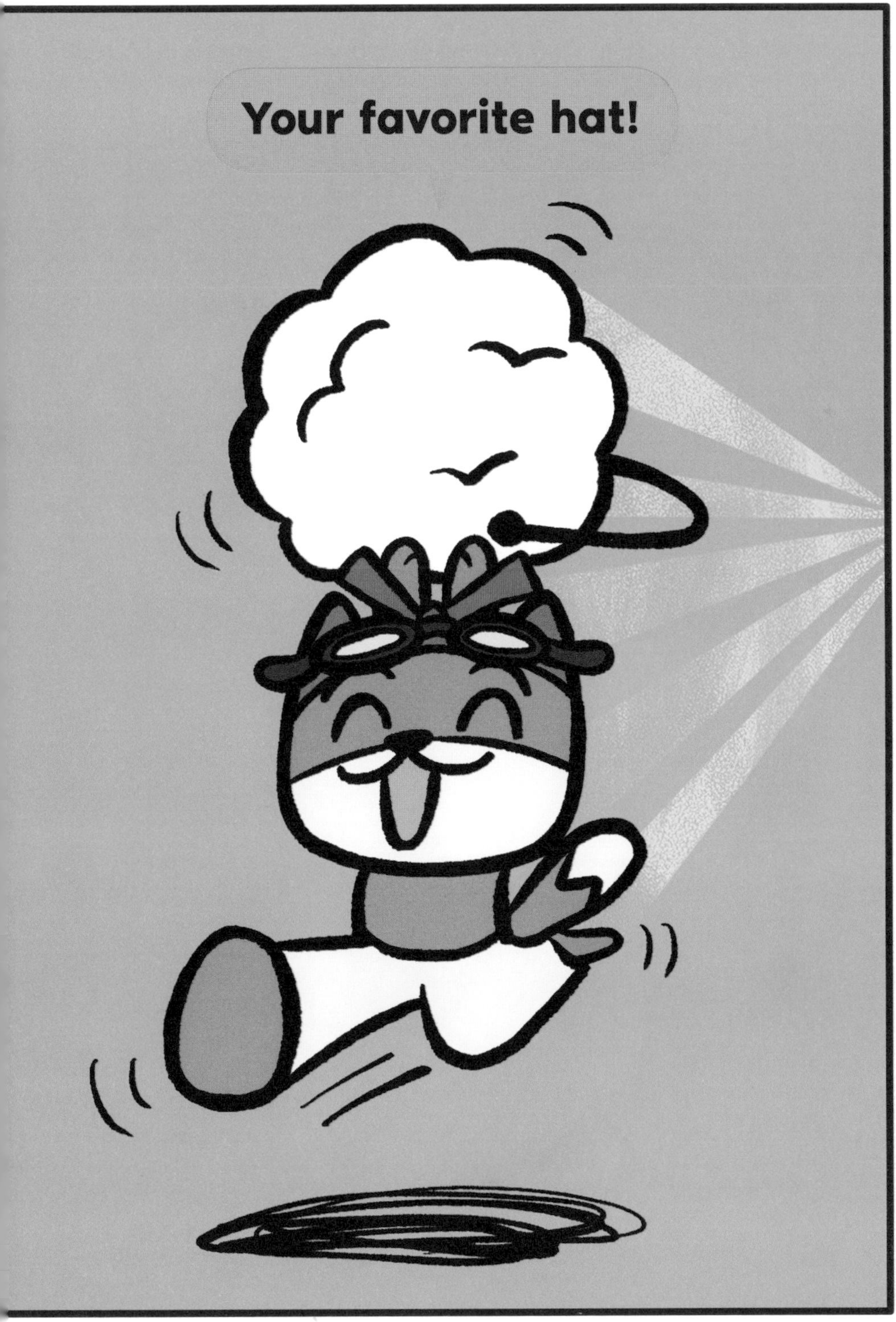
Your favorite hat!

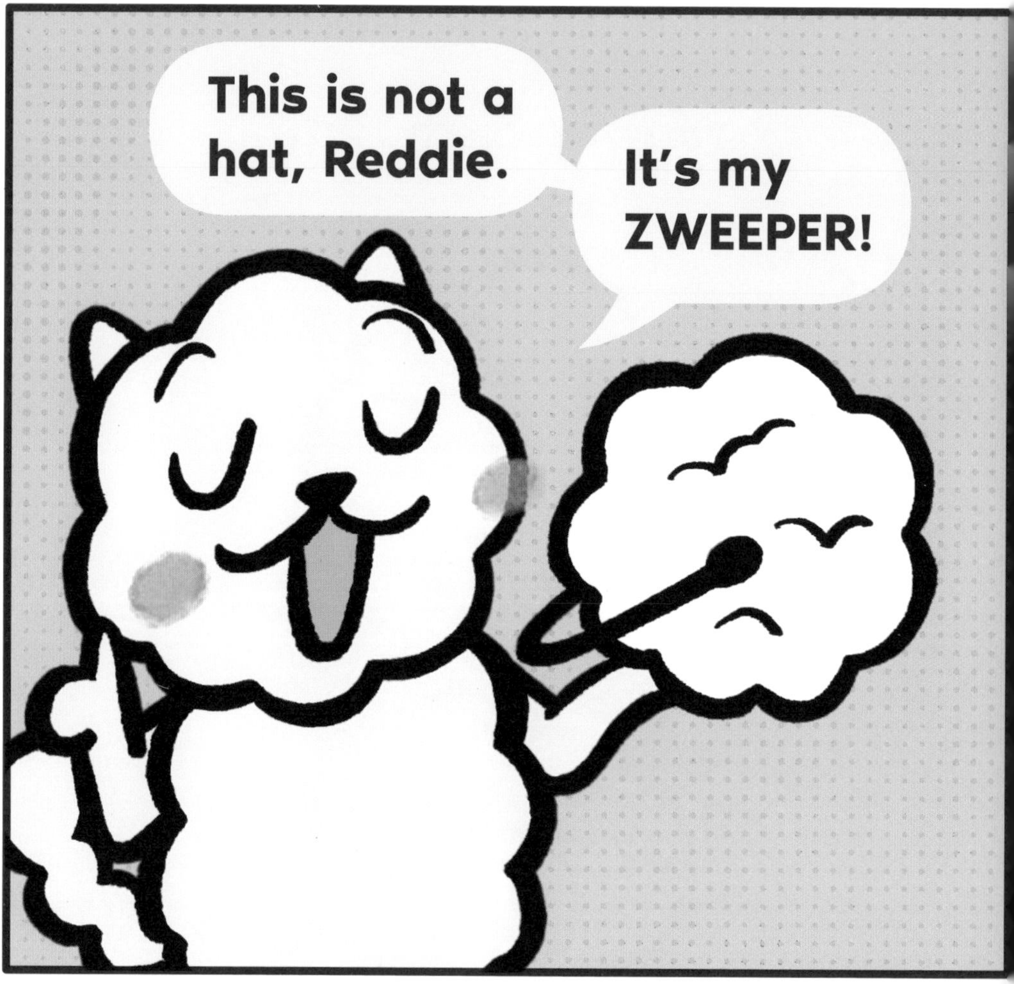
This is not a hat, Reddie.
It's my ZWEEPER!

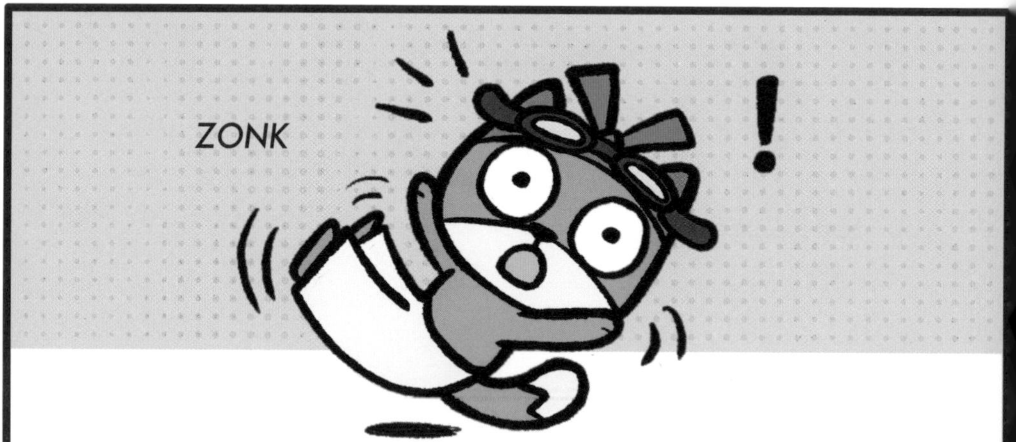
ZONK
!

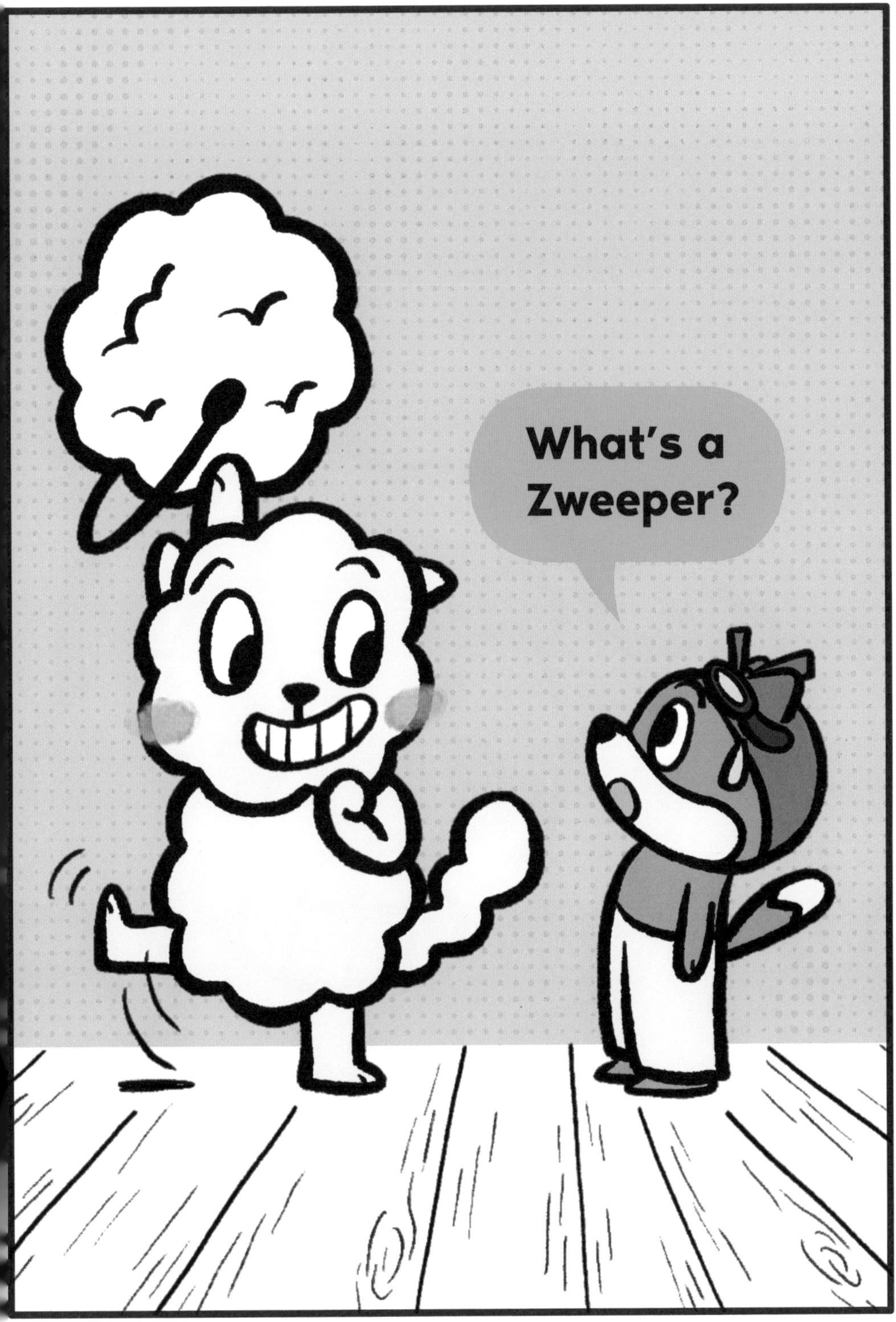
What's a Zweeper?

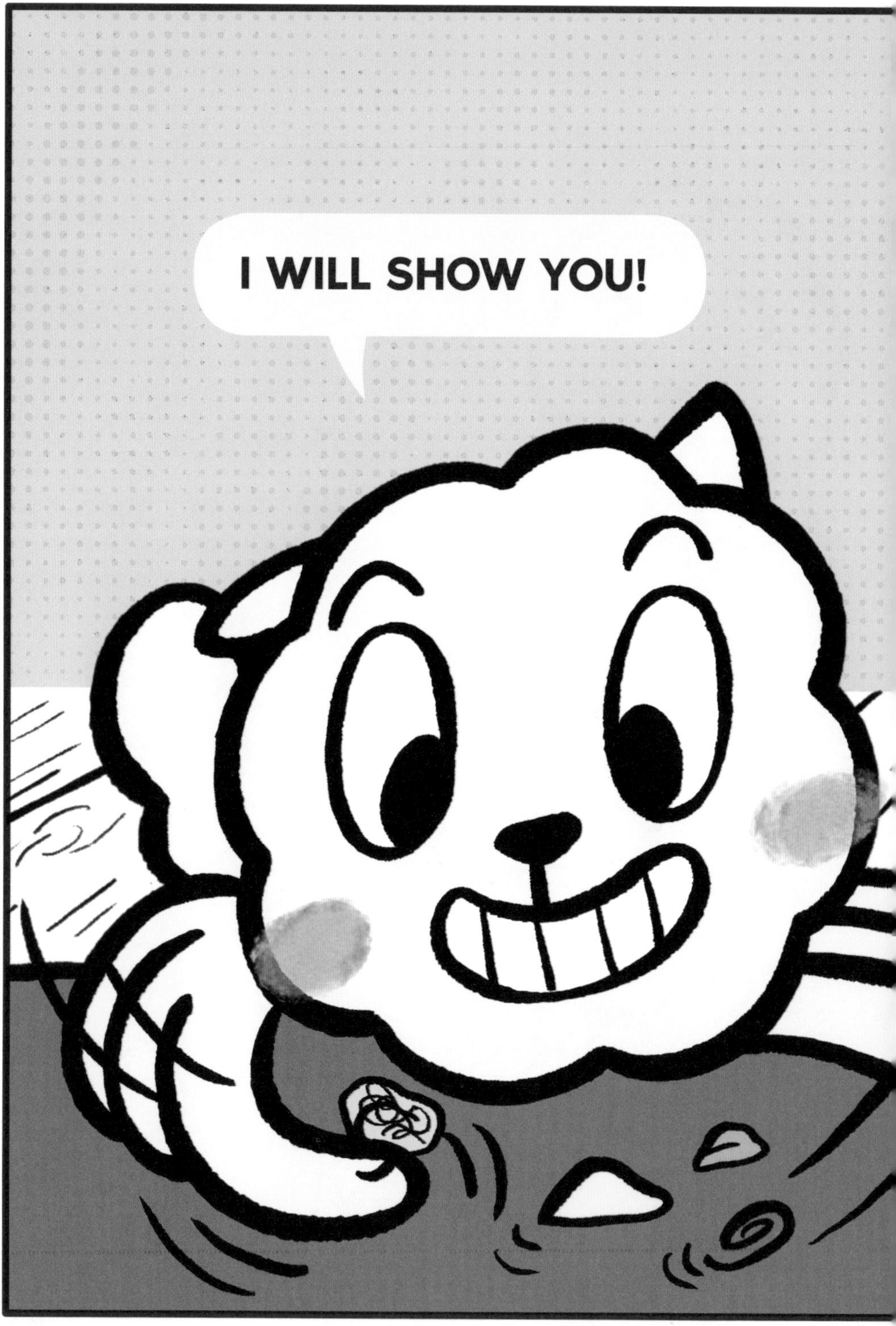
I WILL SHOW YOU!

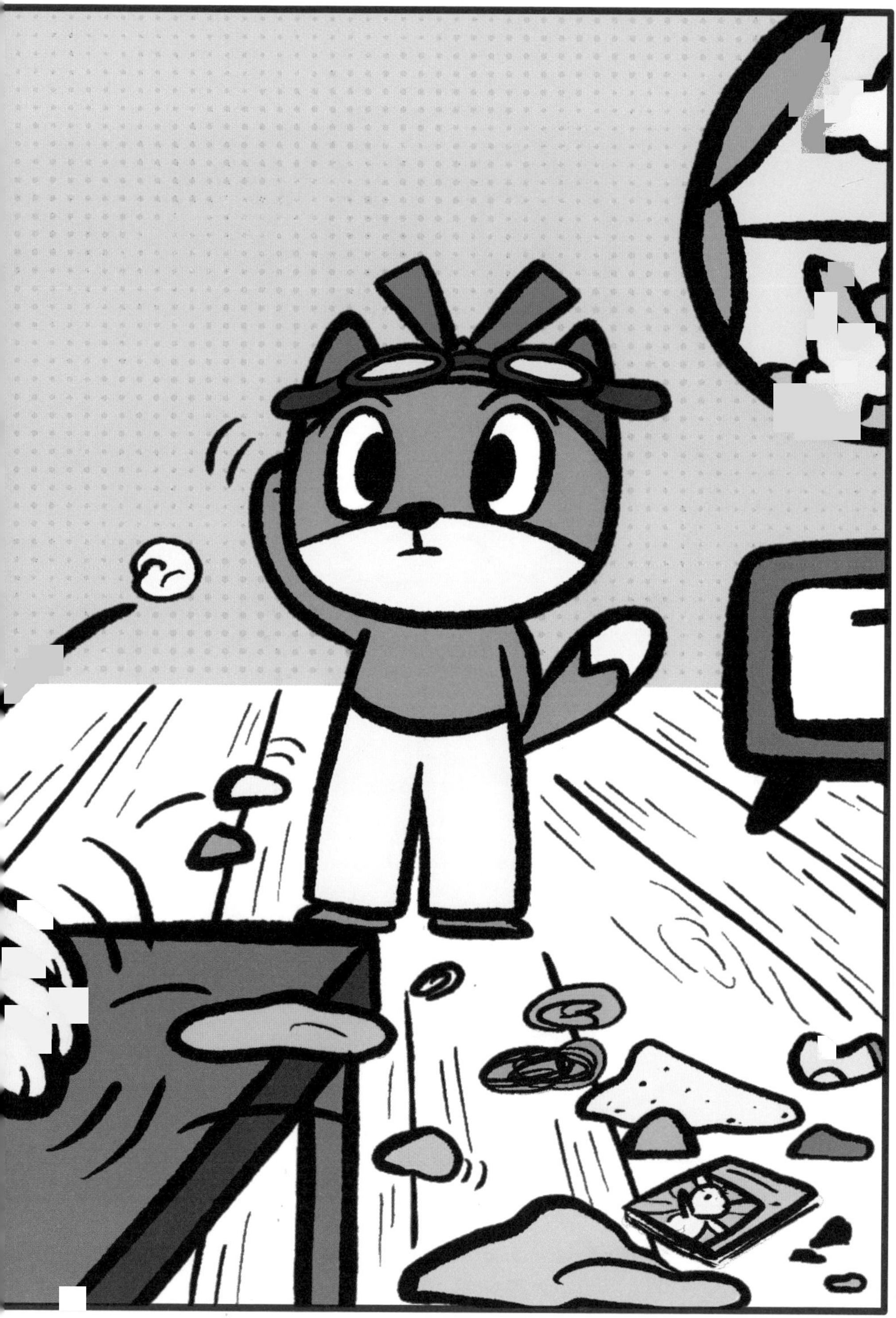

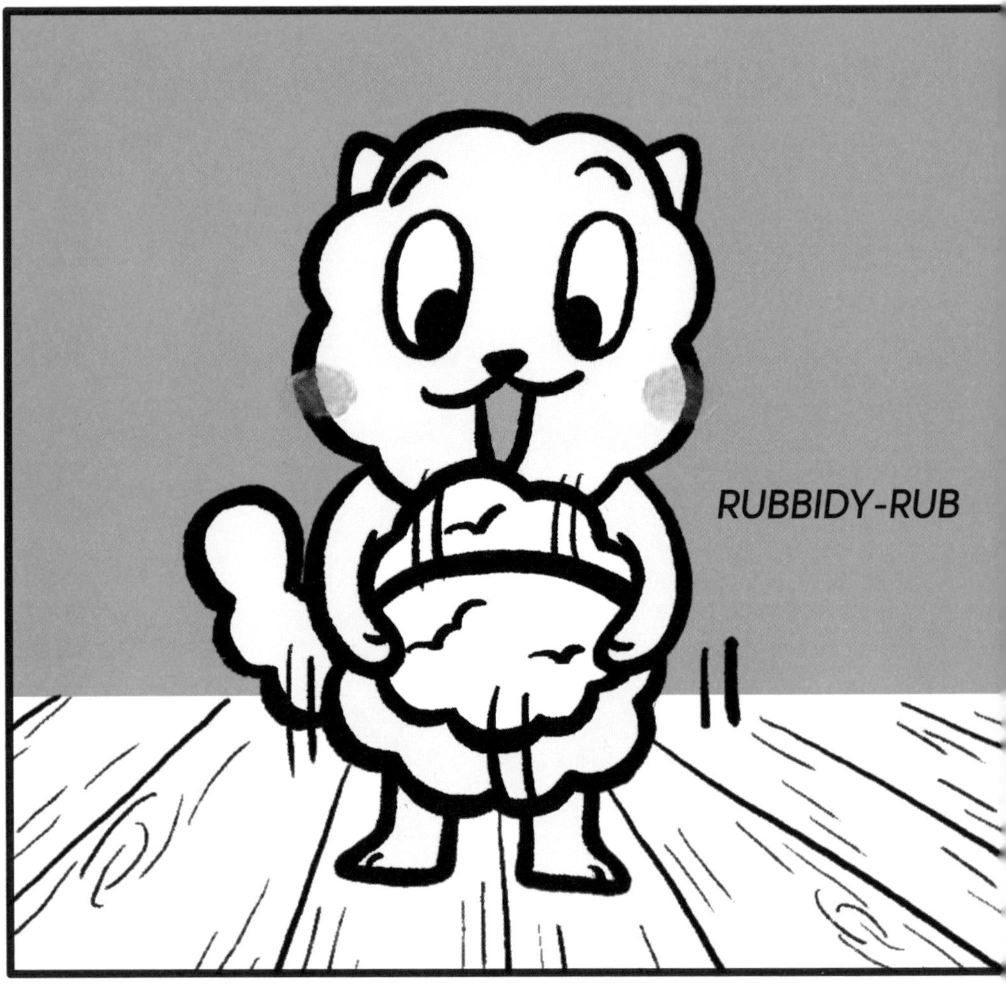
RUBBIDY-RUB

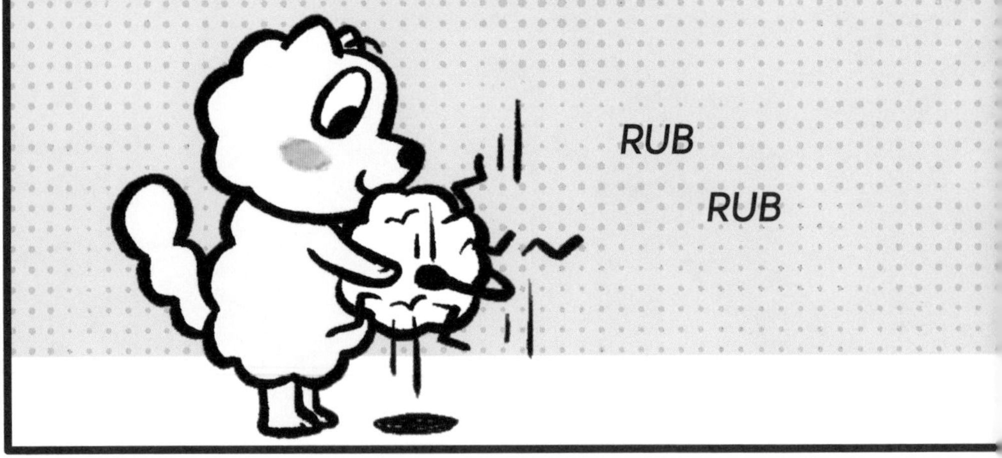
RUB
RUB

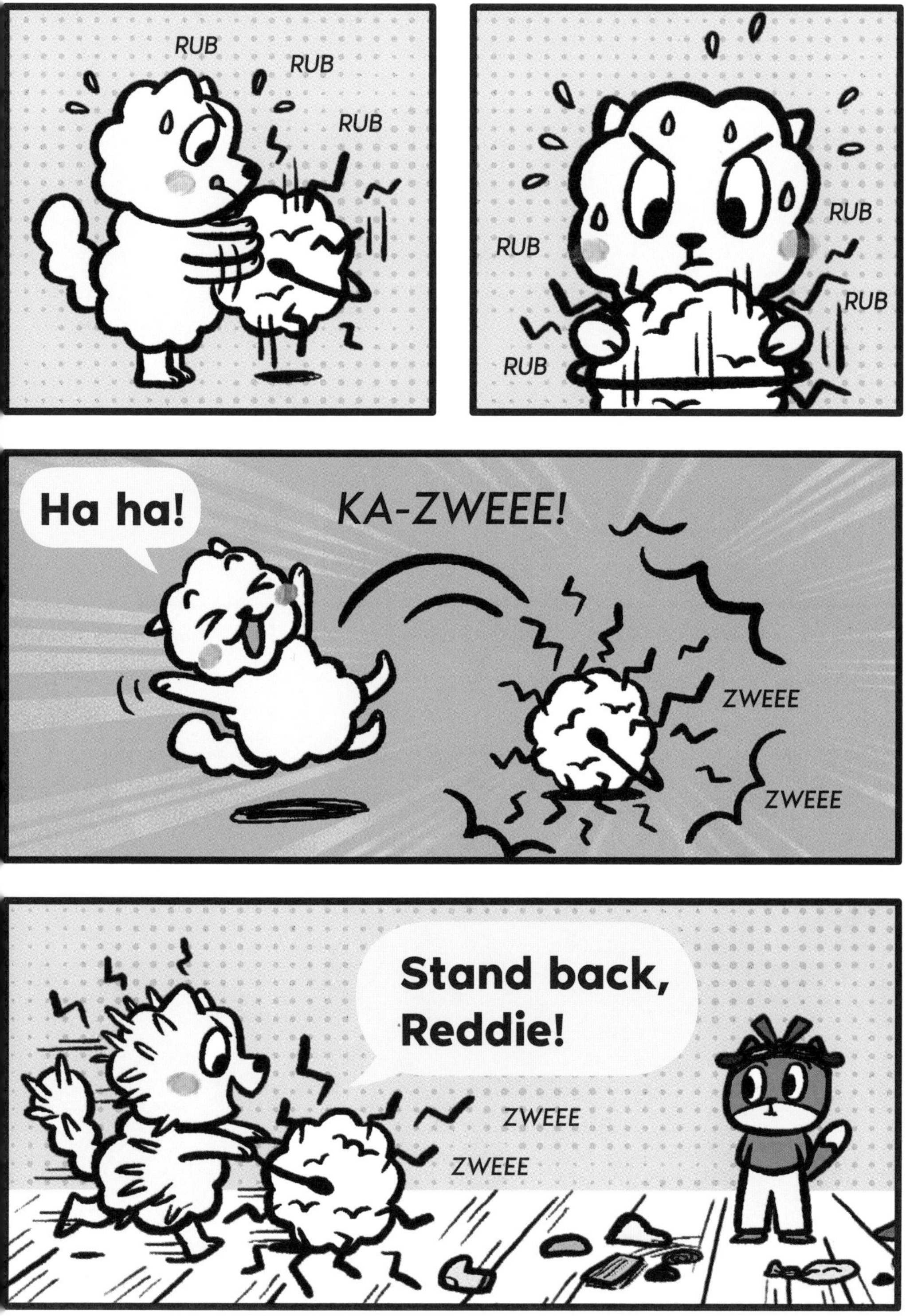
RUB
RUB
RUB
RUB
RUB
RUB
RUB
Ha ha!
KA-ZWEEE!
ZWEEE
ZWEEE
Stand back, Reddie!
ZWEEE
ZWEEE

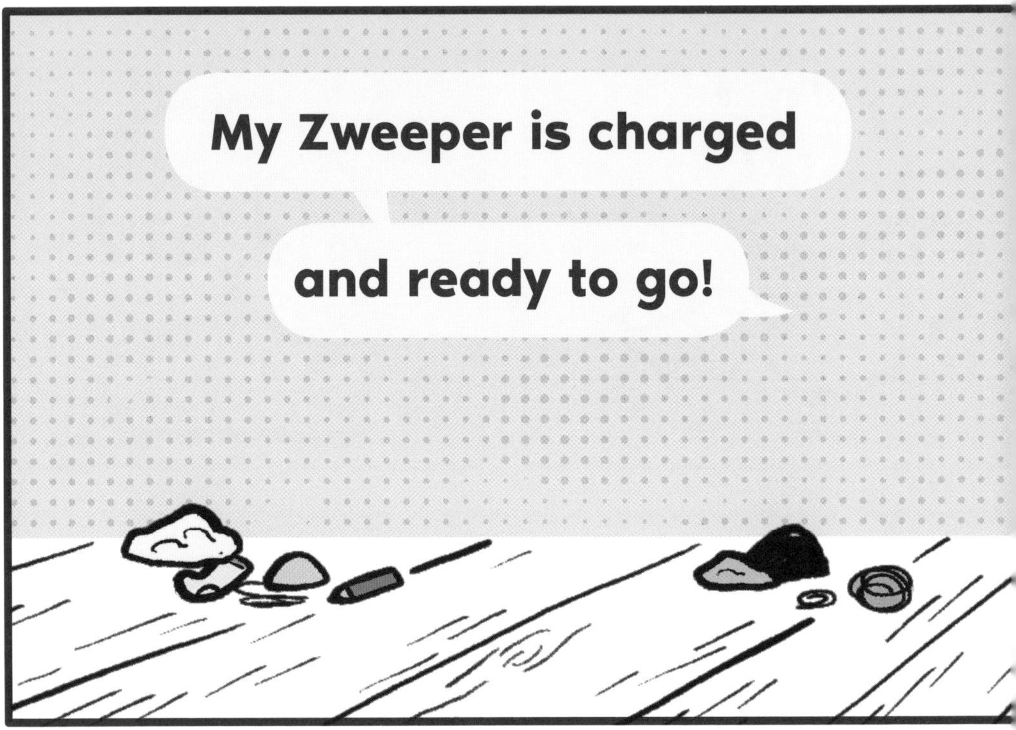
My Zweeper is charged
and ready to go!

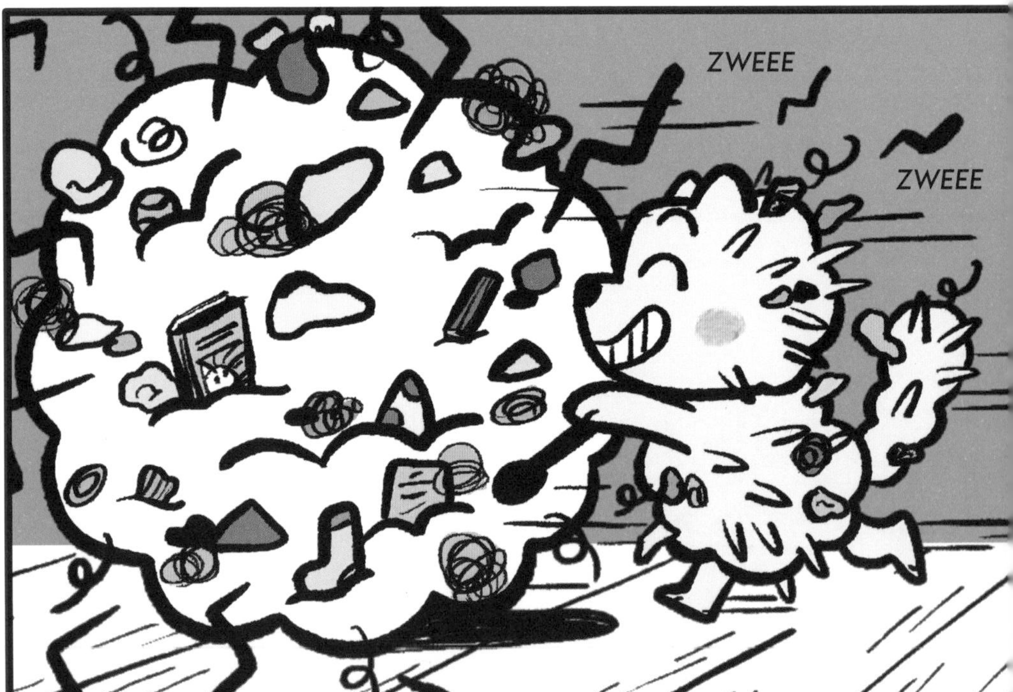
ZWEEE
ZWEEE

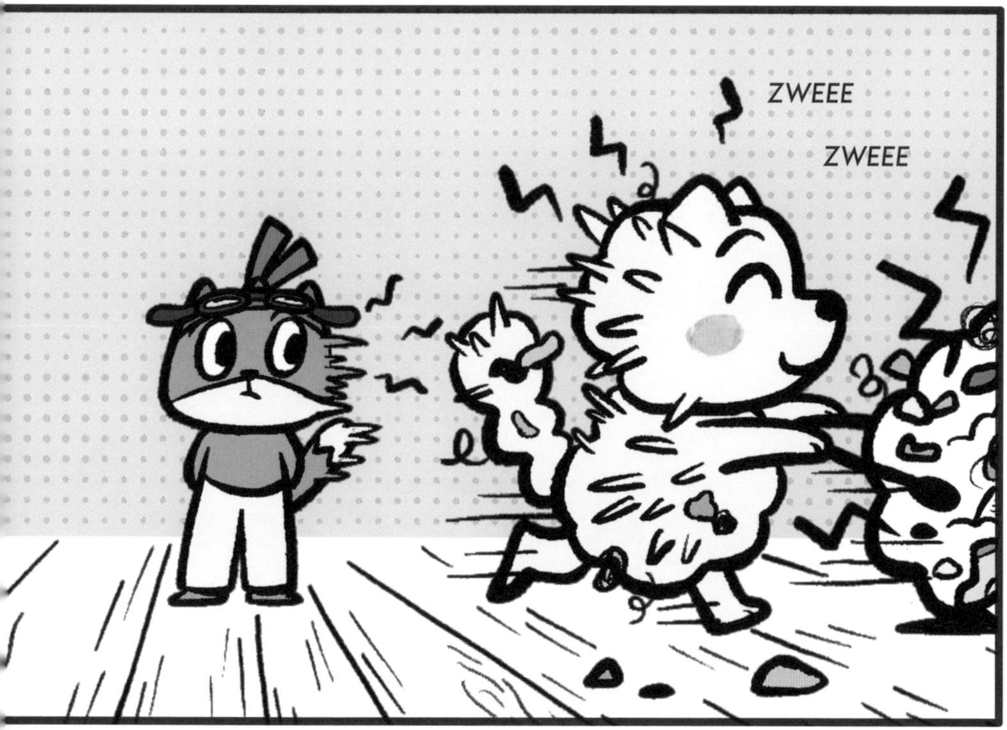
ZWEEE
ZWEEE

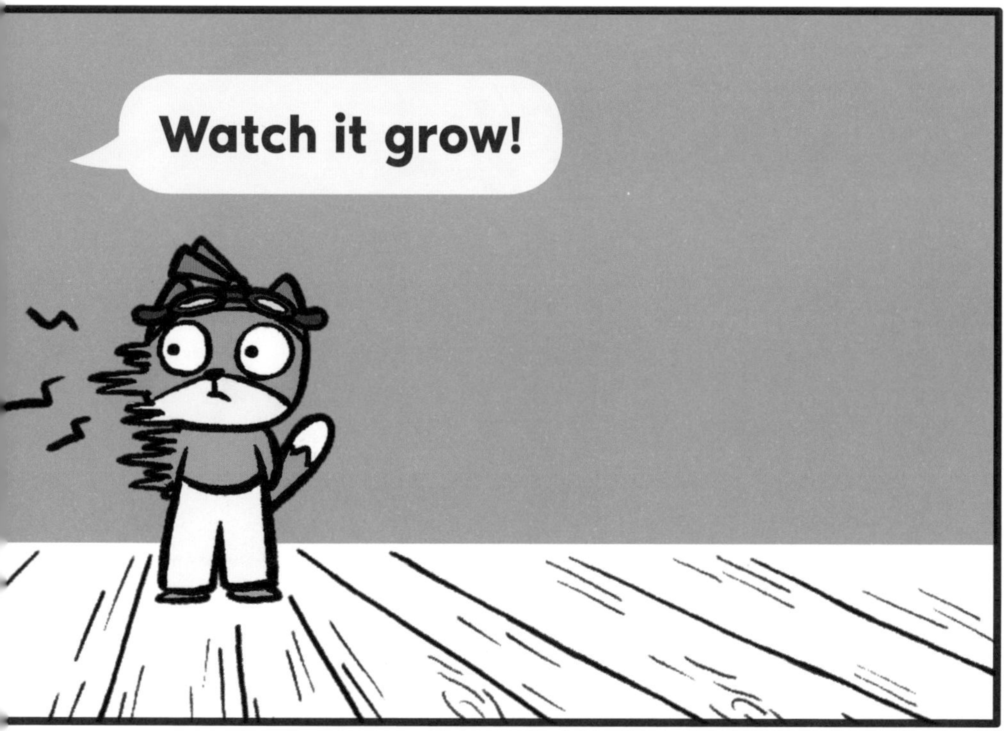
Watch it grow!

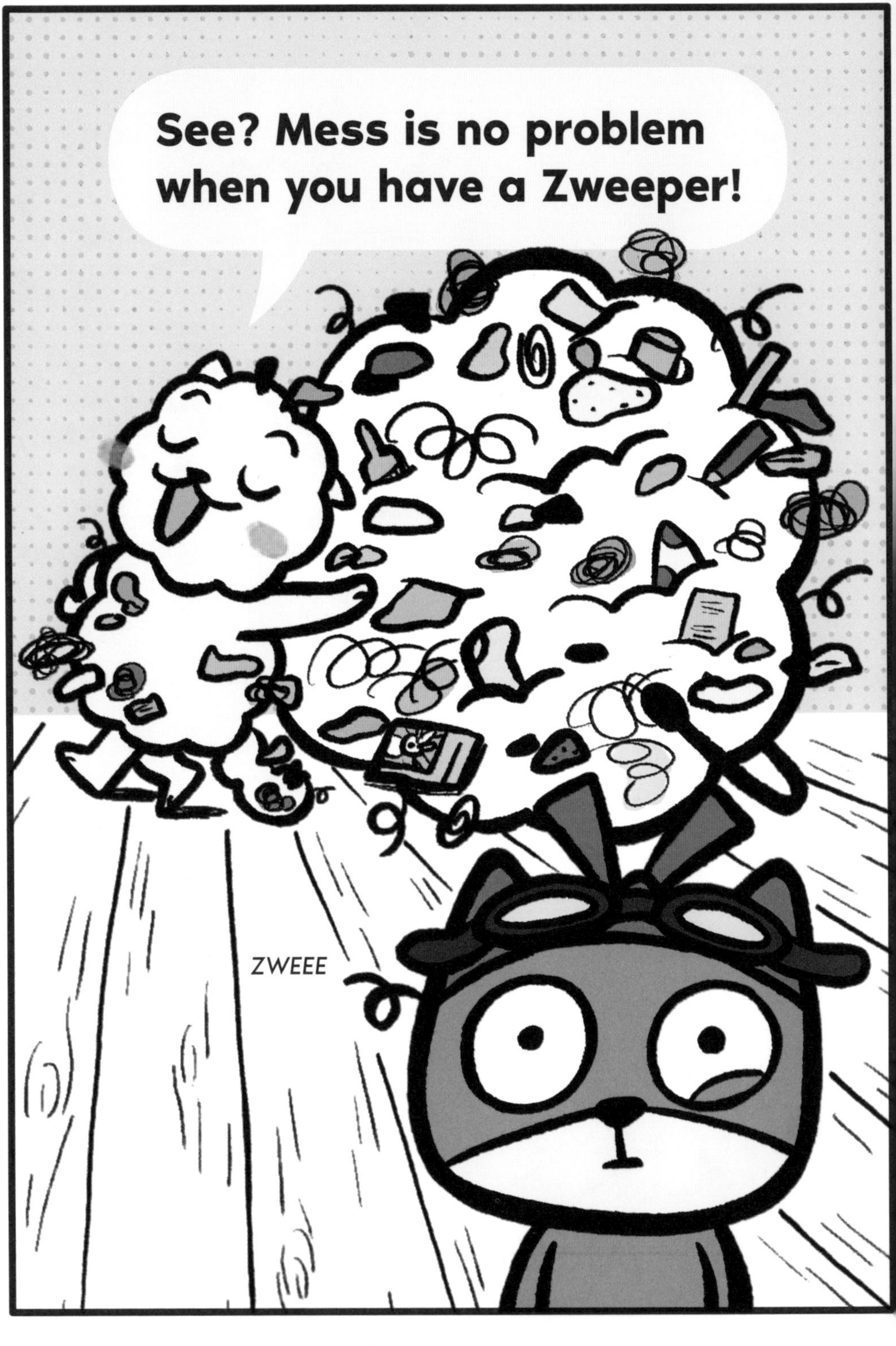
See? Mess is no problem when you have a Zweeper!
ZWEEE

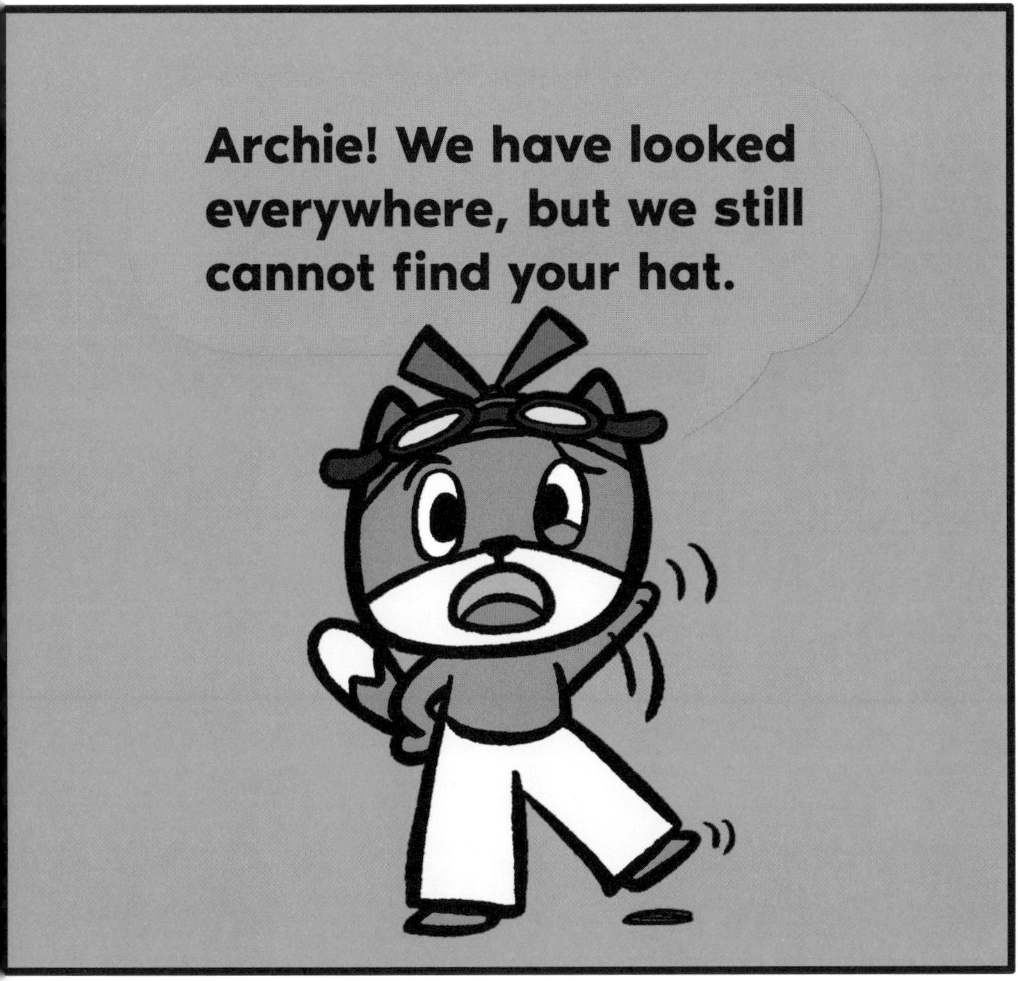
Archie! We have looked everywhere, but we still cannot find your hat.

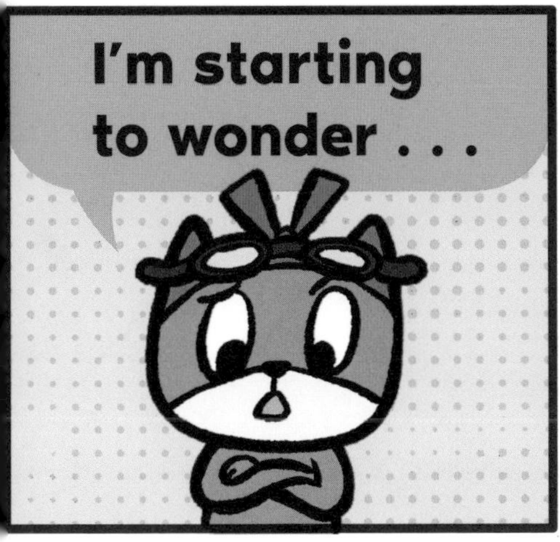
I'm starting to wonder . . .

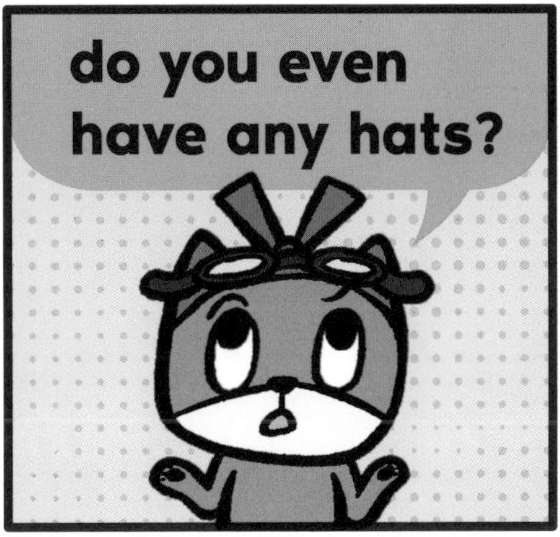
do you even have any hats?

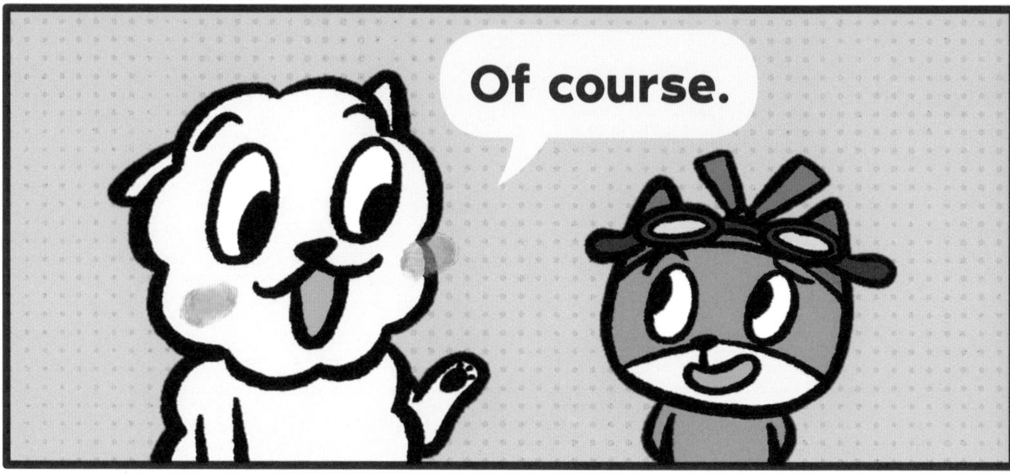
Of course.

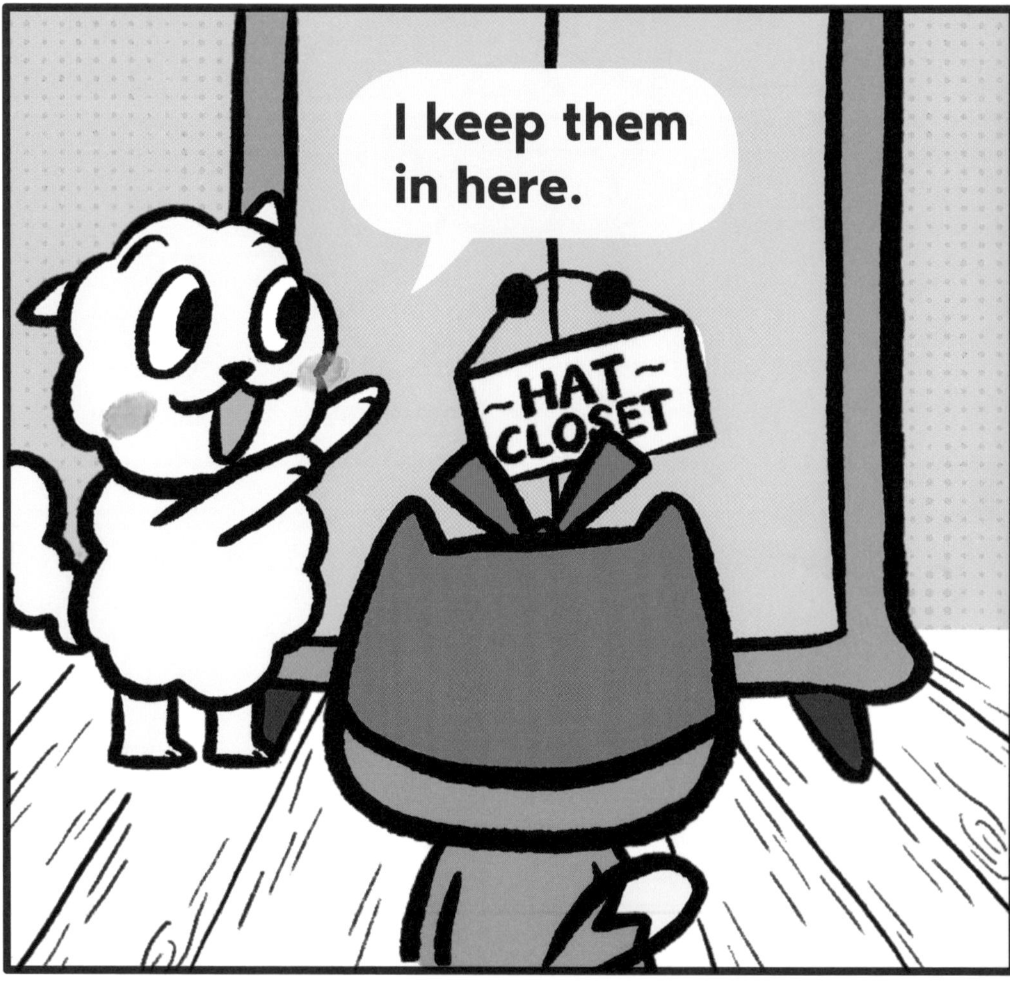
I keep them in here.
~HAT~
CLOSET

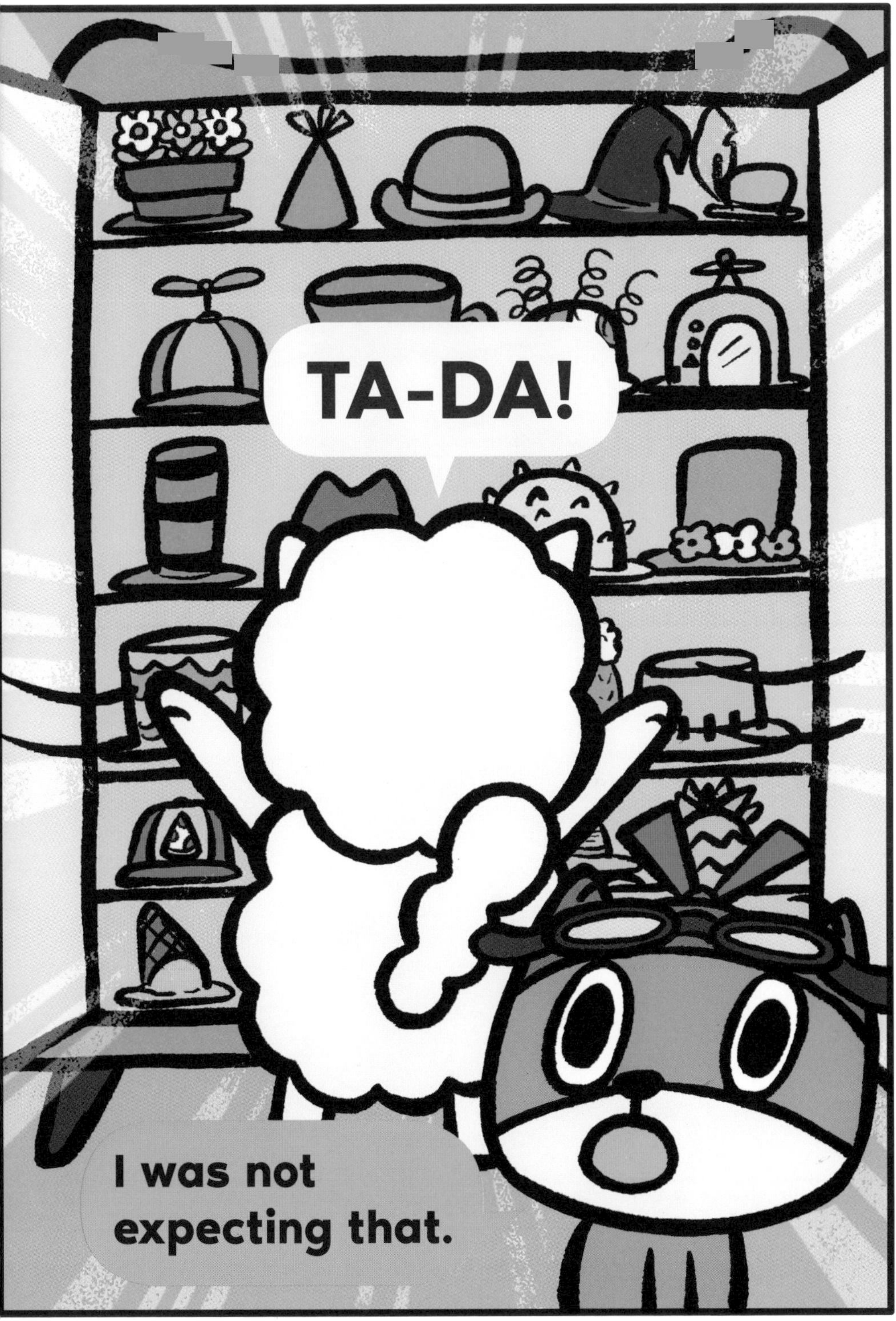
TA-DA!
I was not expecting that.

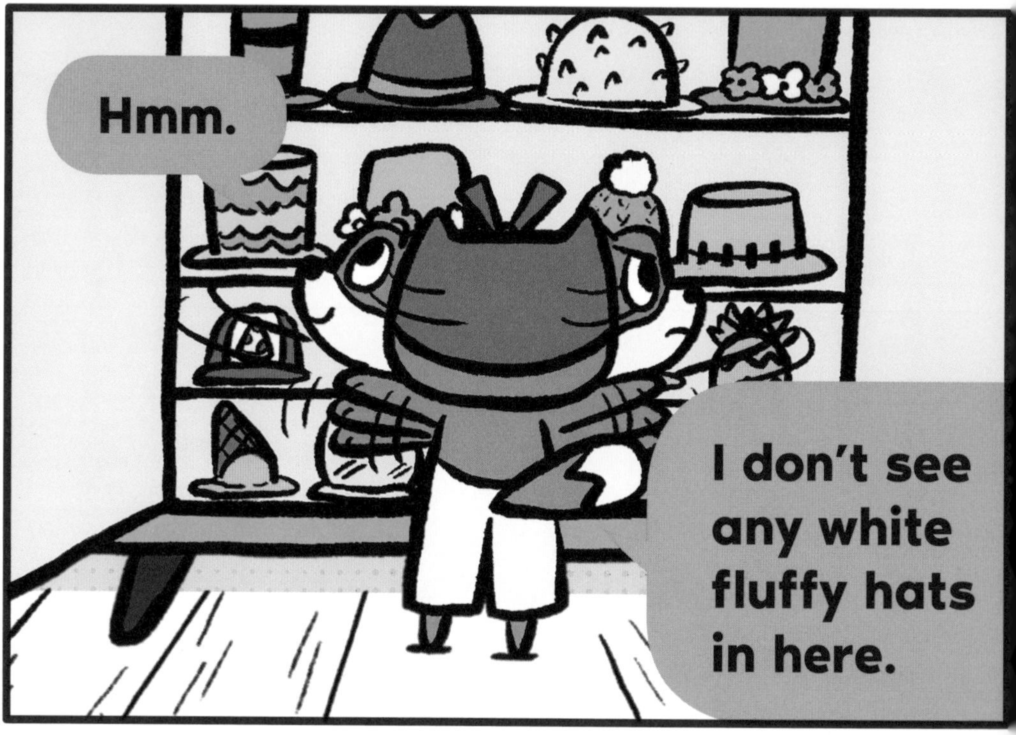
Hmm.
I don't see any white fluffy hats in here.

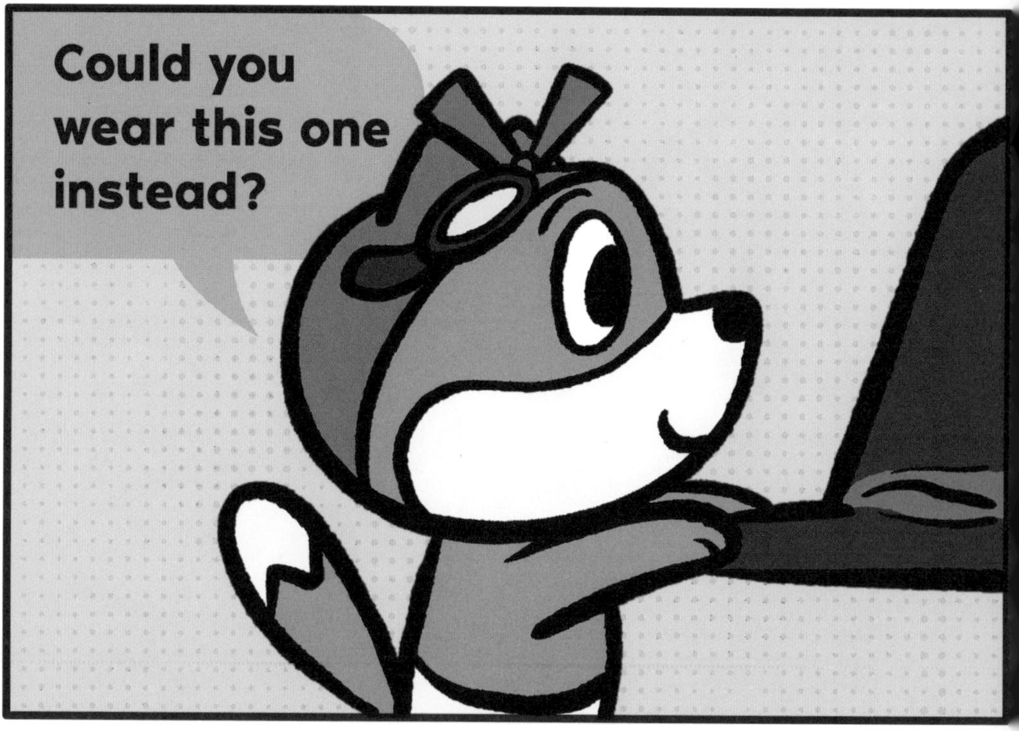
Could you wear this one instead?

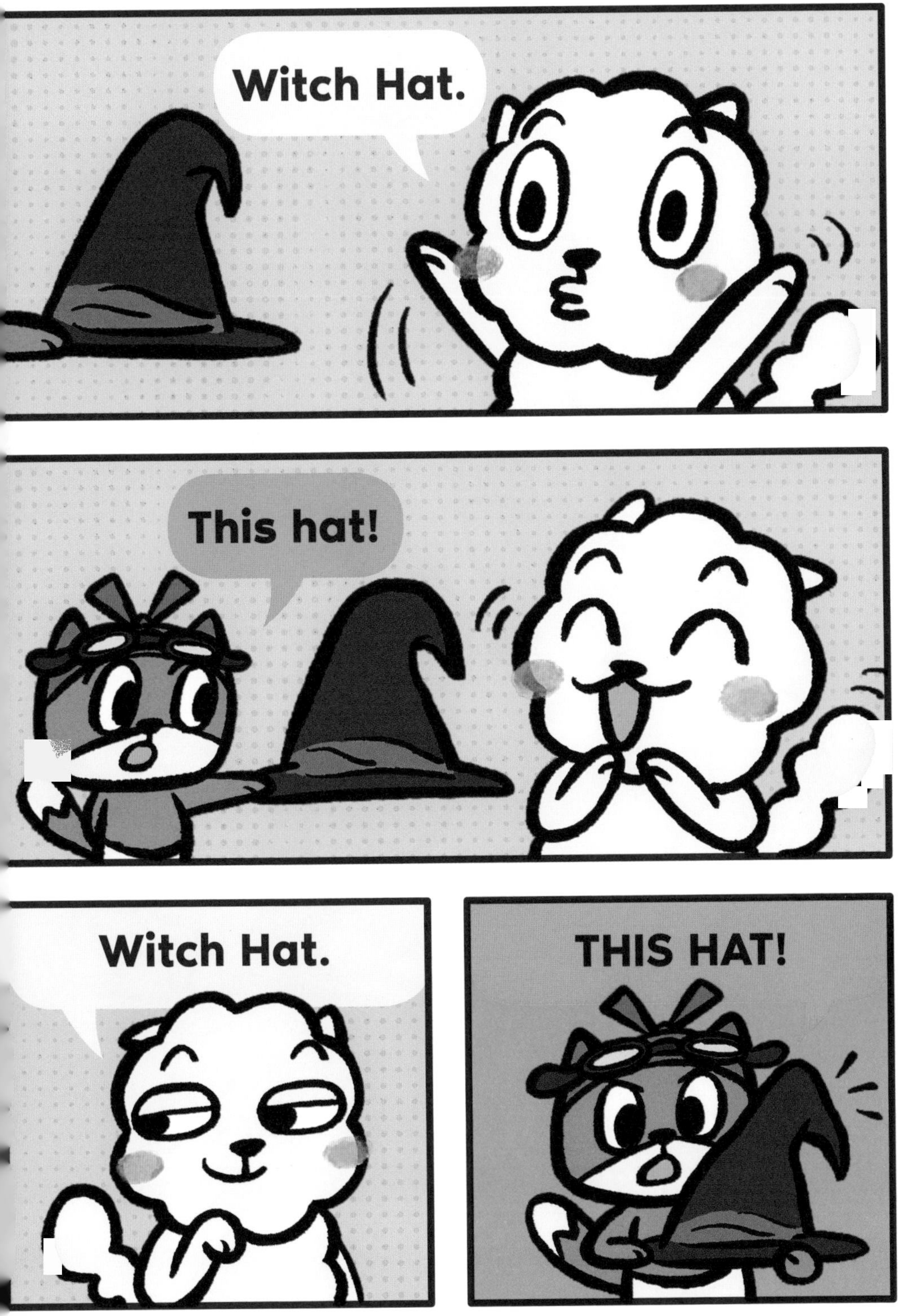
Witch Hat.
This hat!
Witch Hat.
THIS HAT!

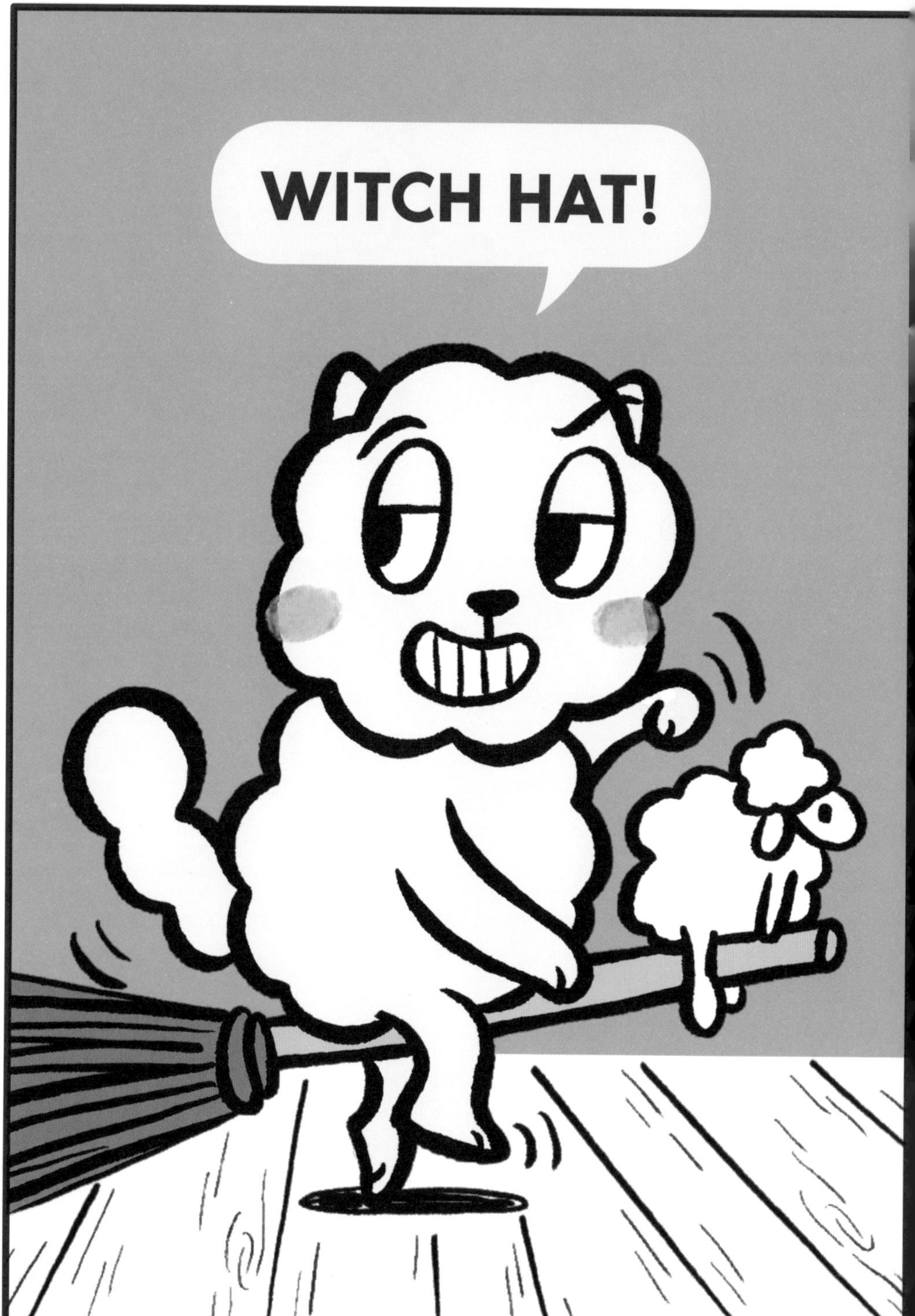
WITCH HAT!

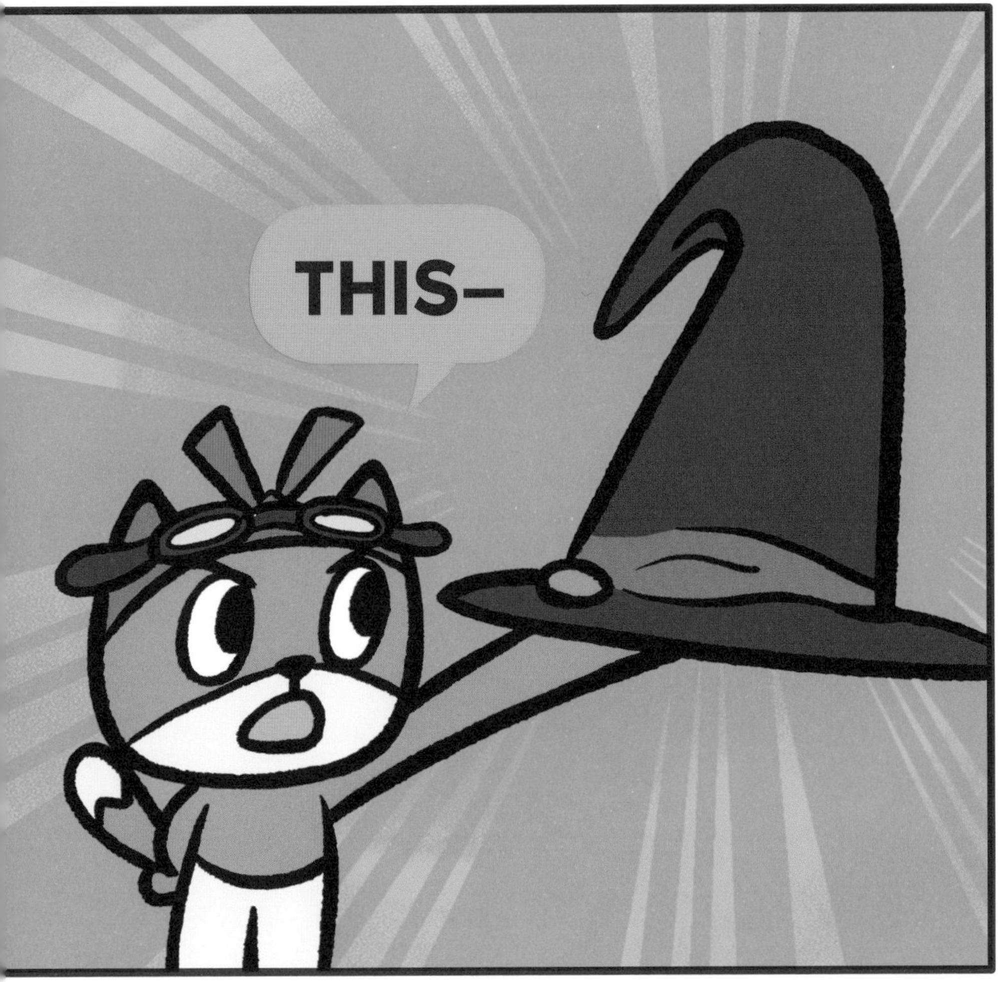
THIS–

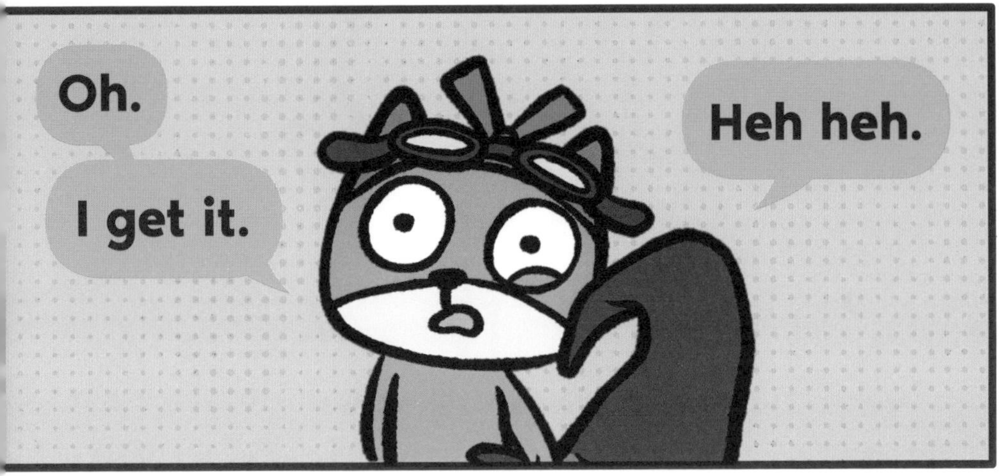
Oh.
I get it.
Heh heh.

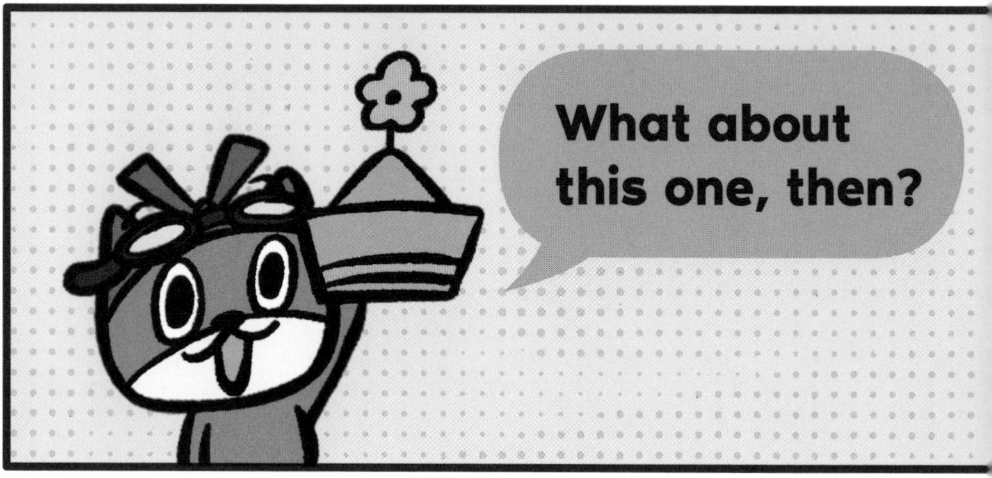
What about
this one, then?

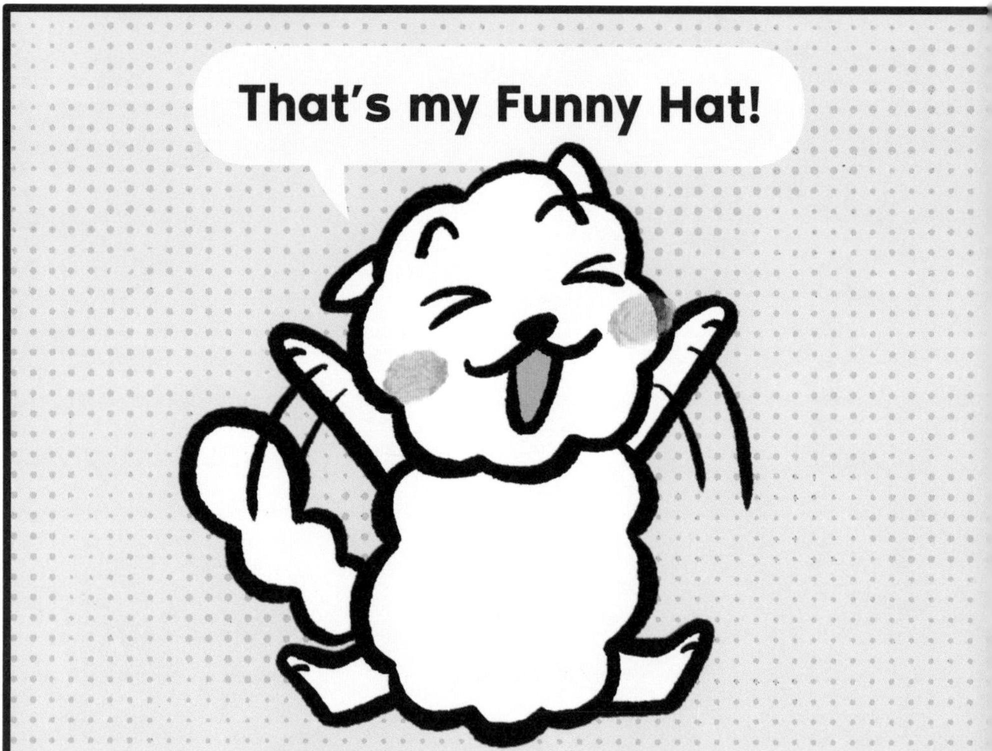
That's my Funny Hat!

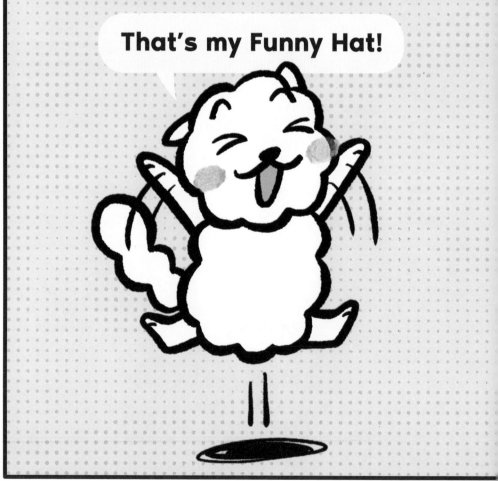

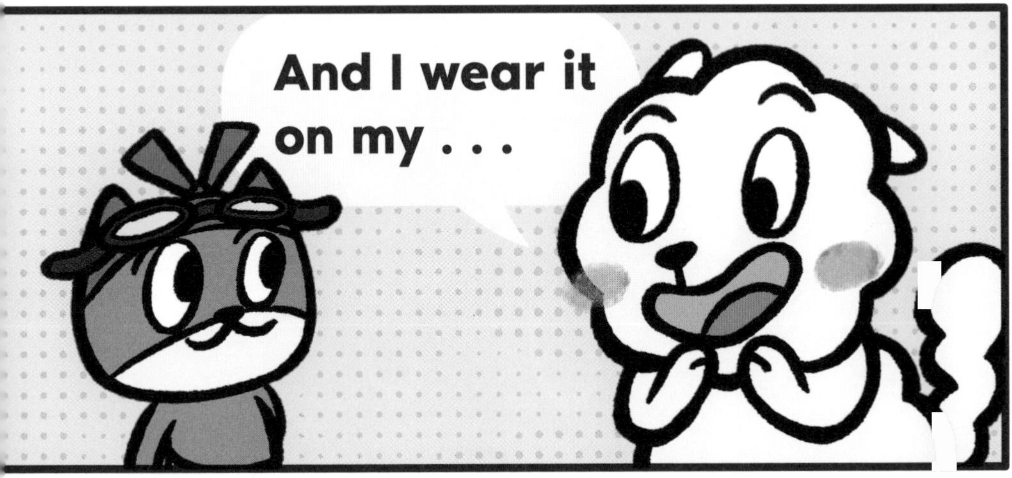
And I wear it on my . . .

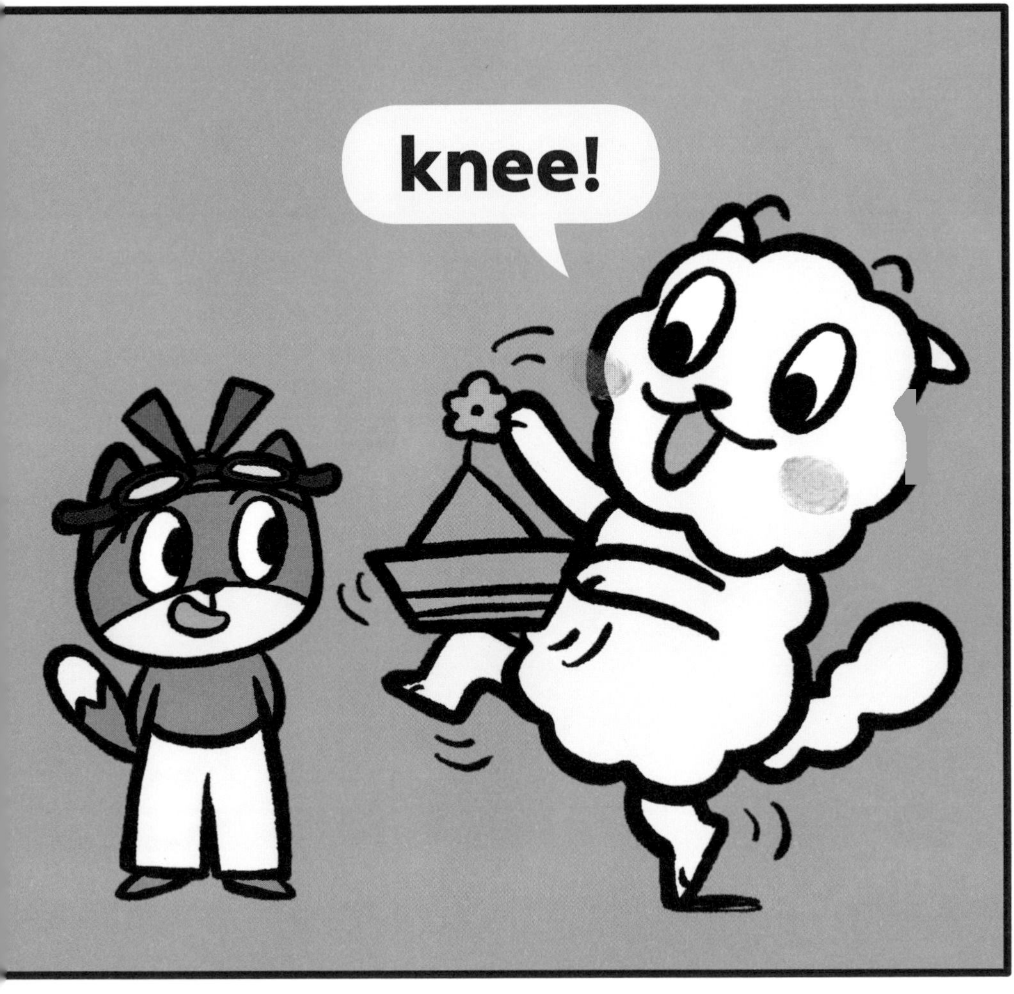
knee!

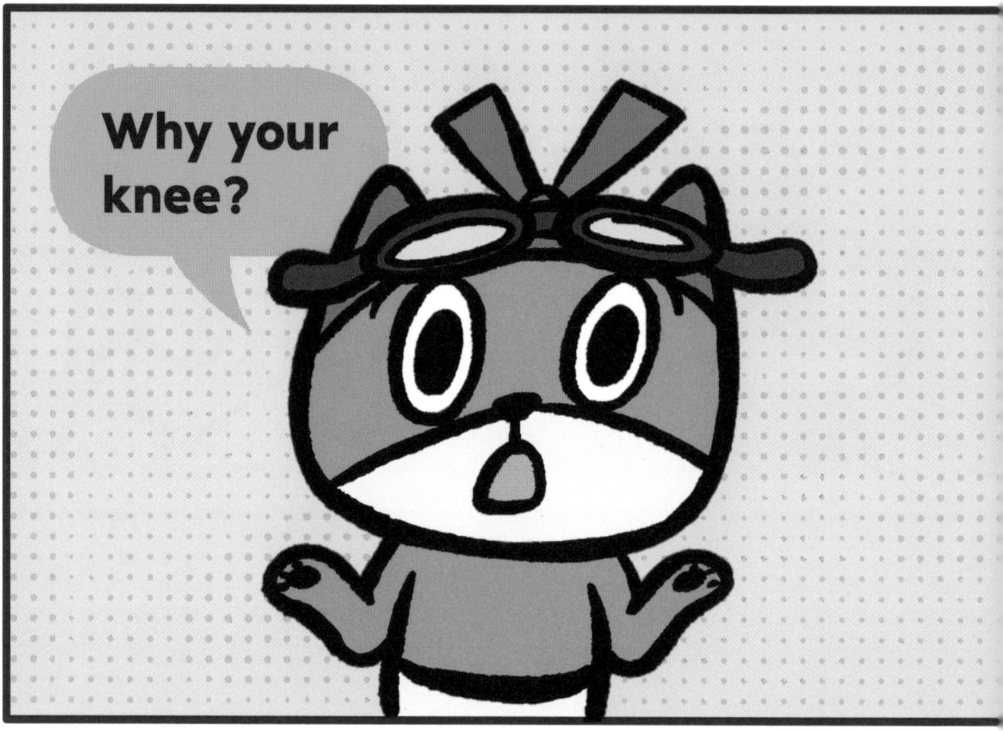
Why your knee?

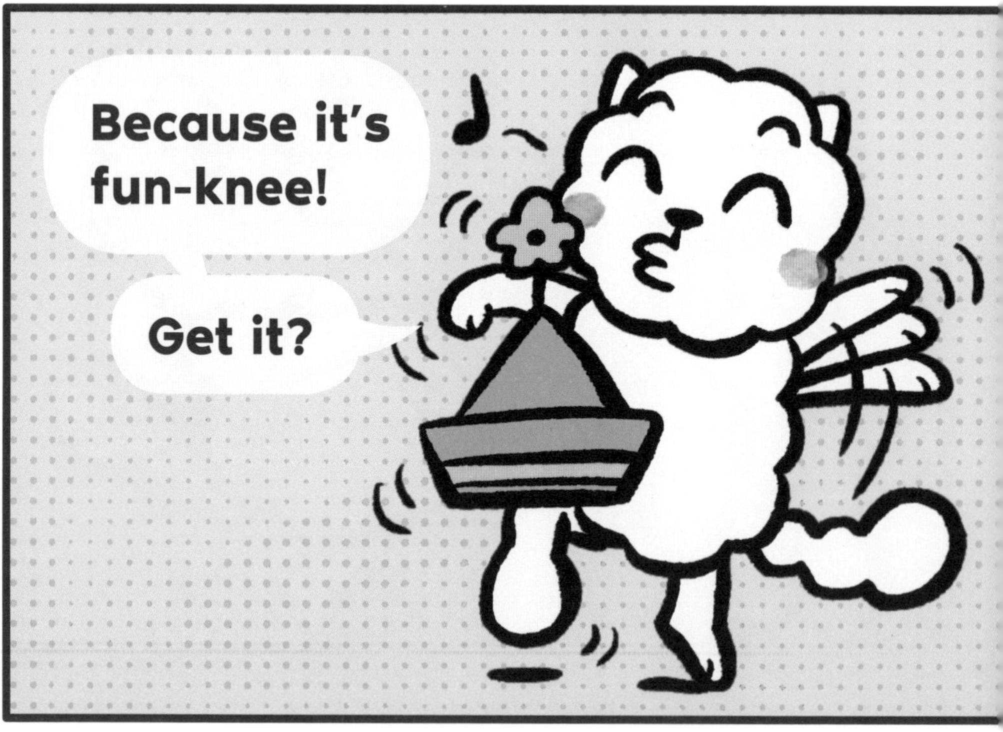
Because it's fun-knee!
Get it?

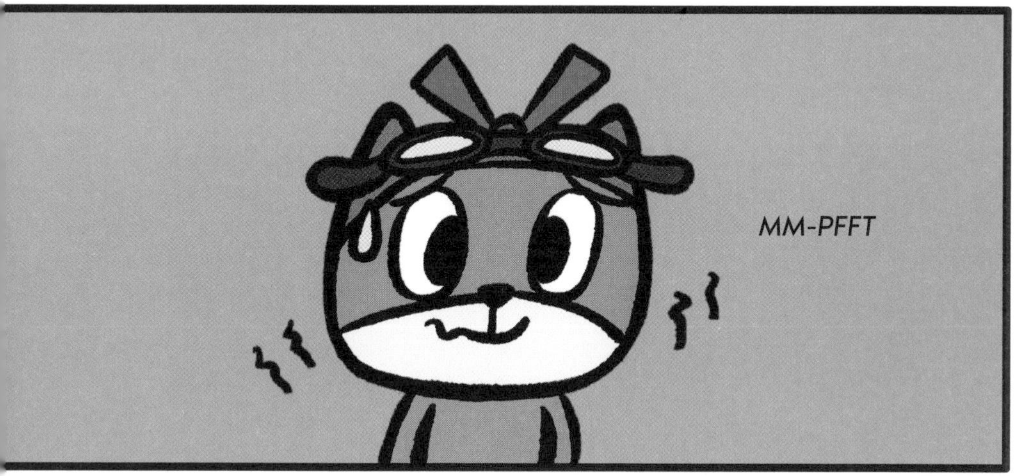
MM-PFFT

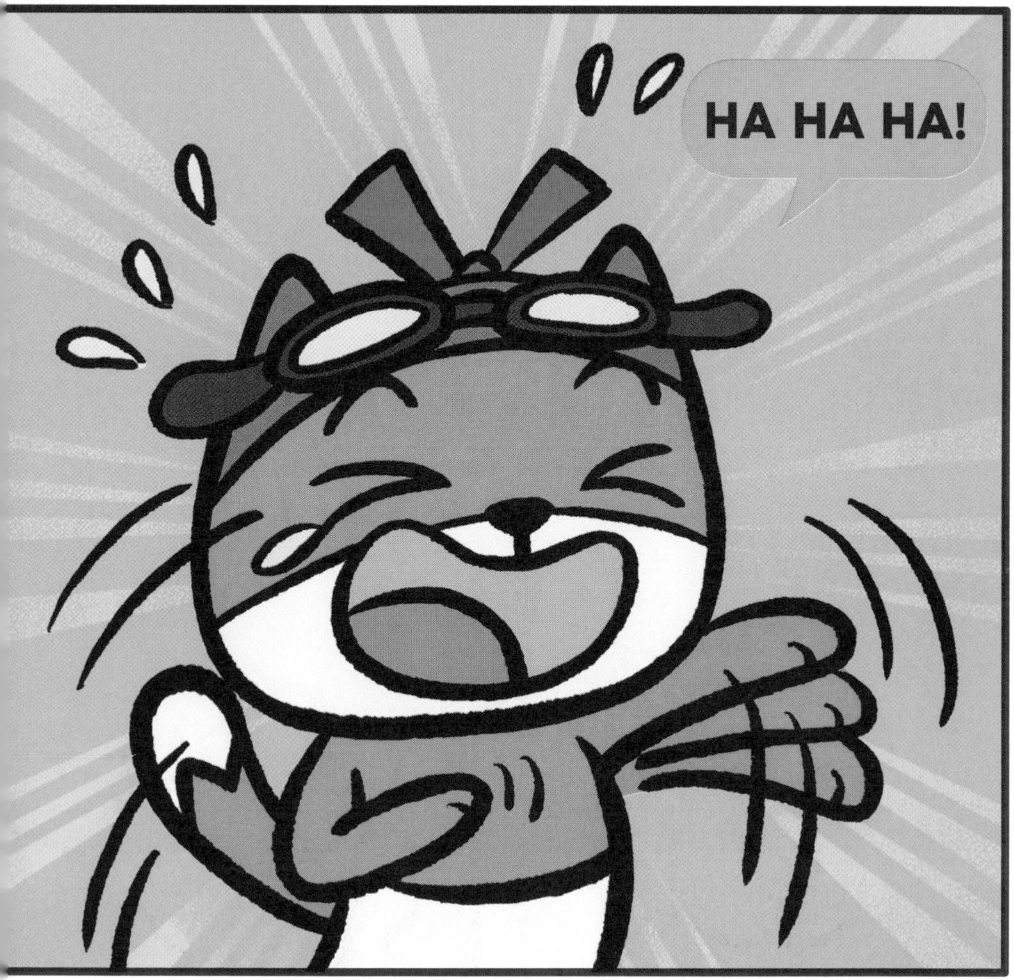
HA HA HA!

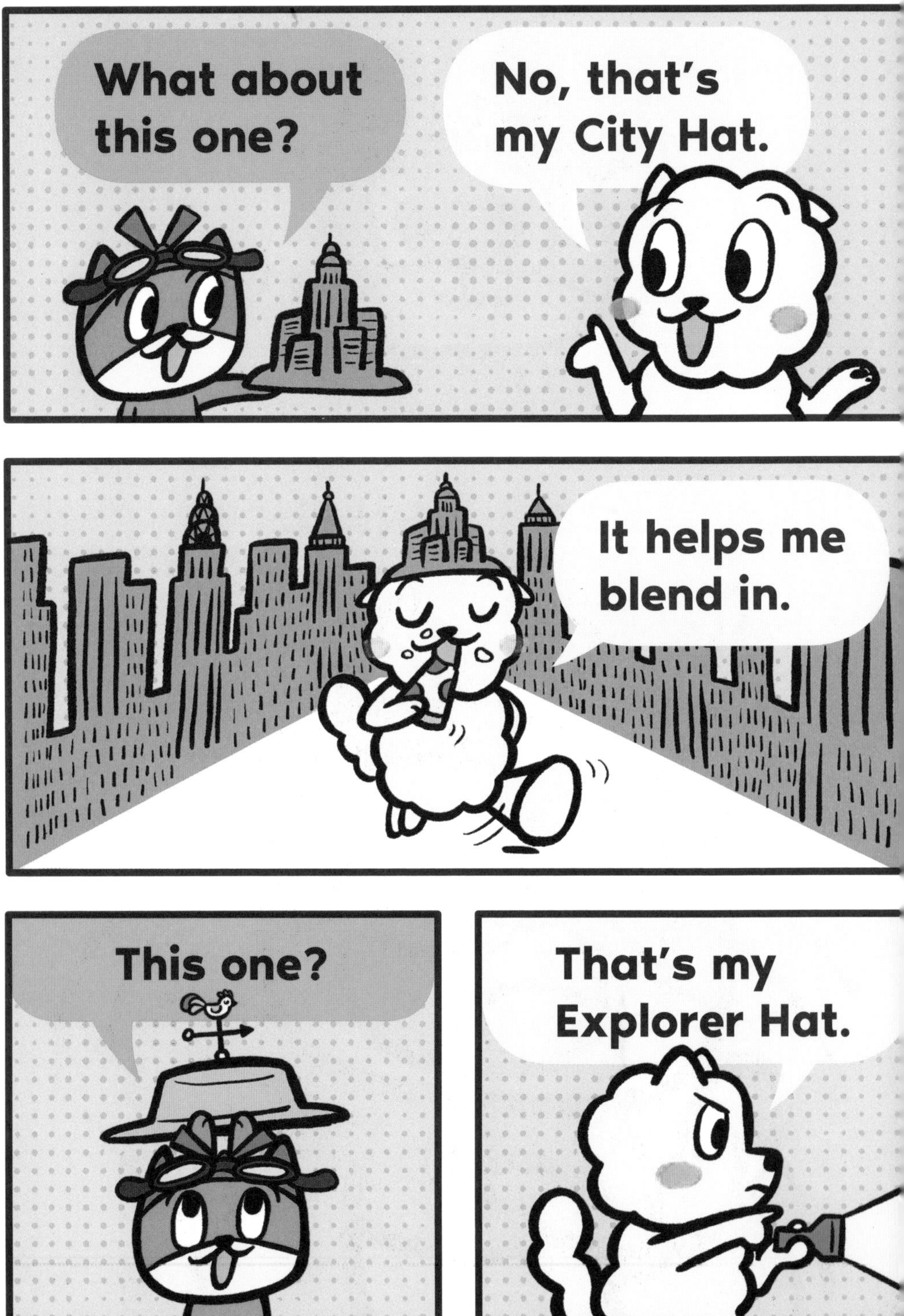
What about this one?
No, that's my City Hat.
It helps me blend in.
This one?
That's my Explorer Hat.

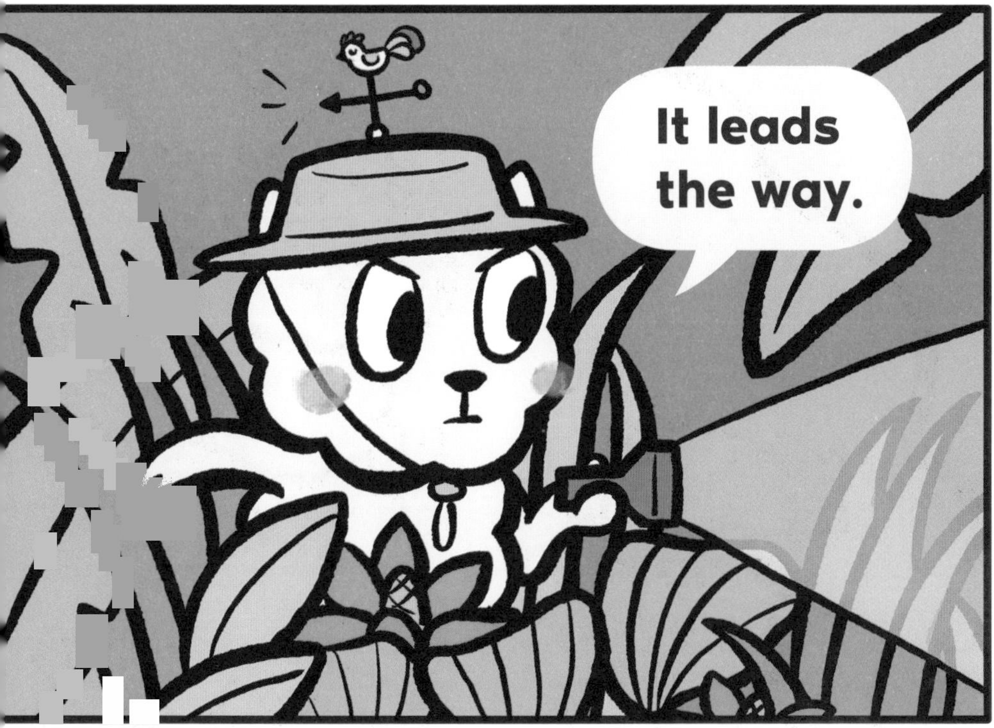
It leads the way.

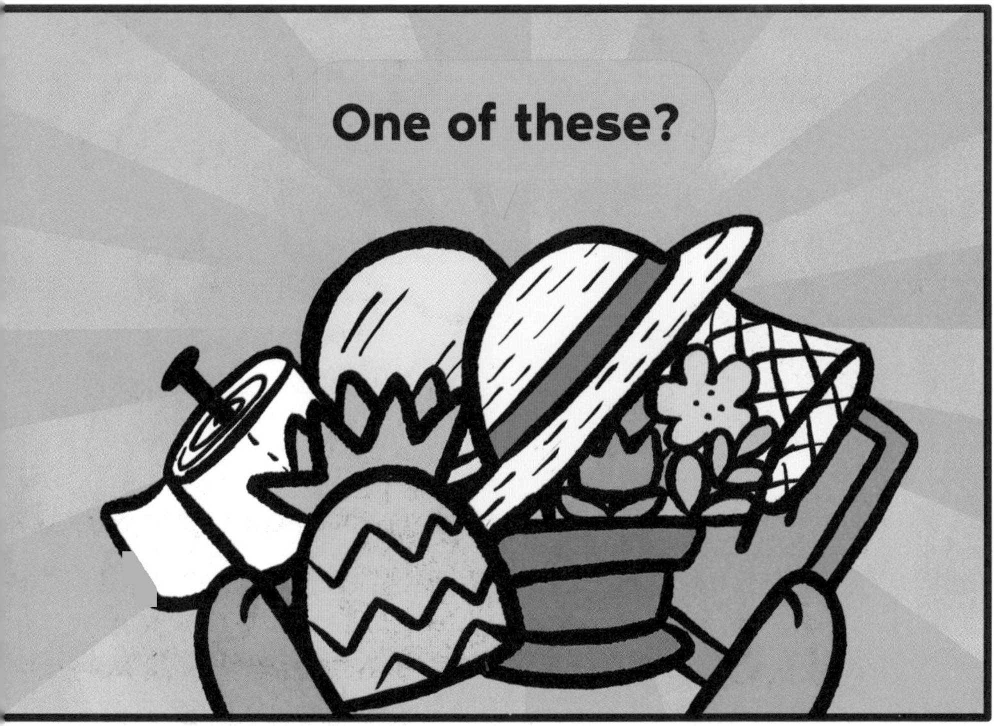
One of these?

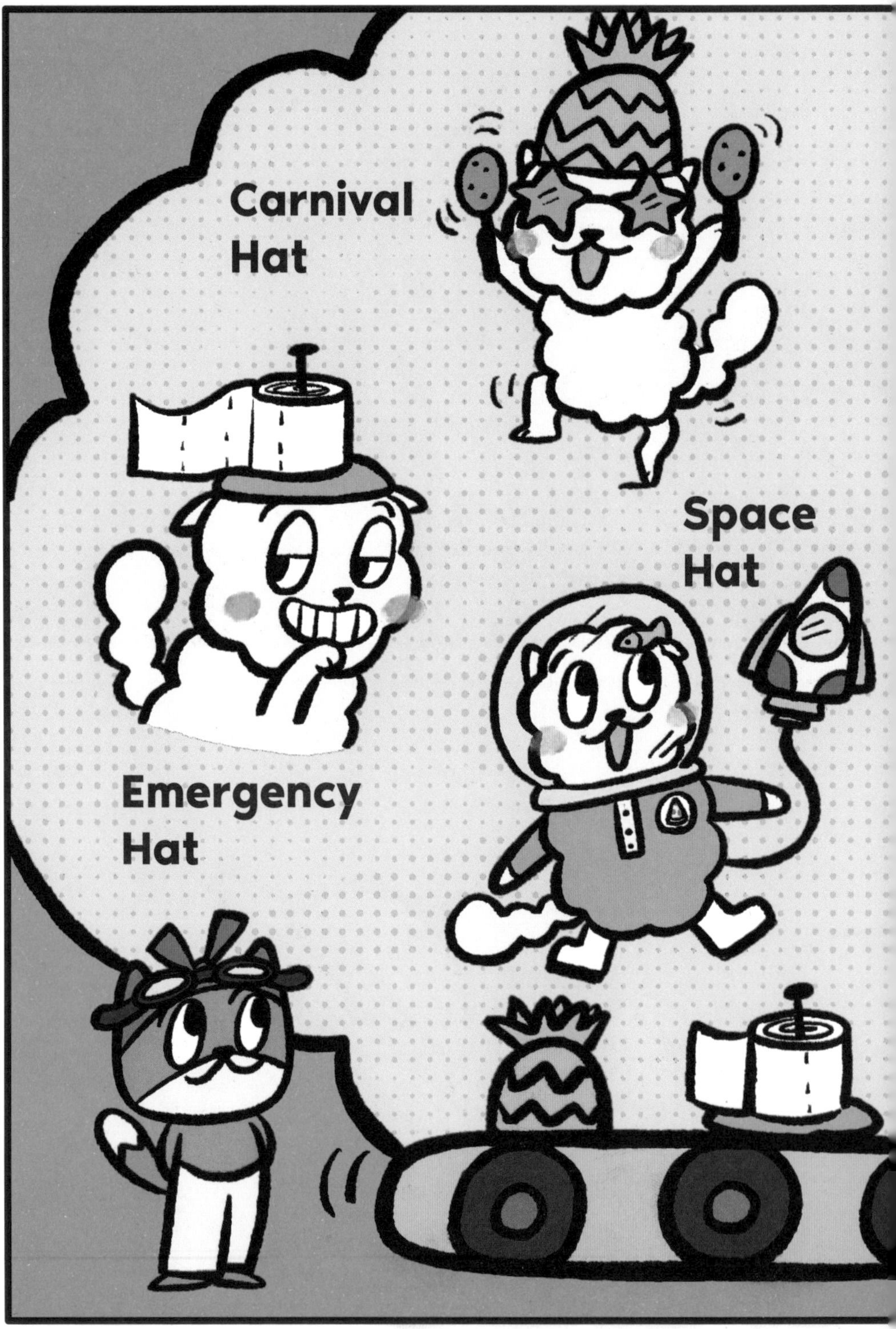
Carnival Hat
Space Hat
Emergency Hat

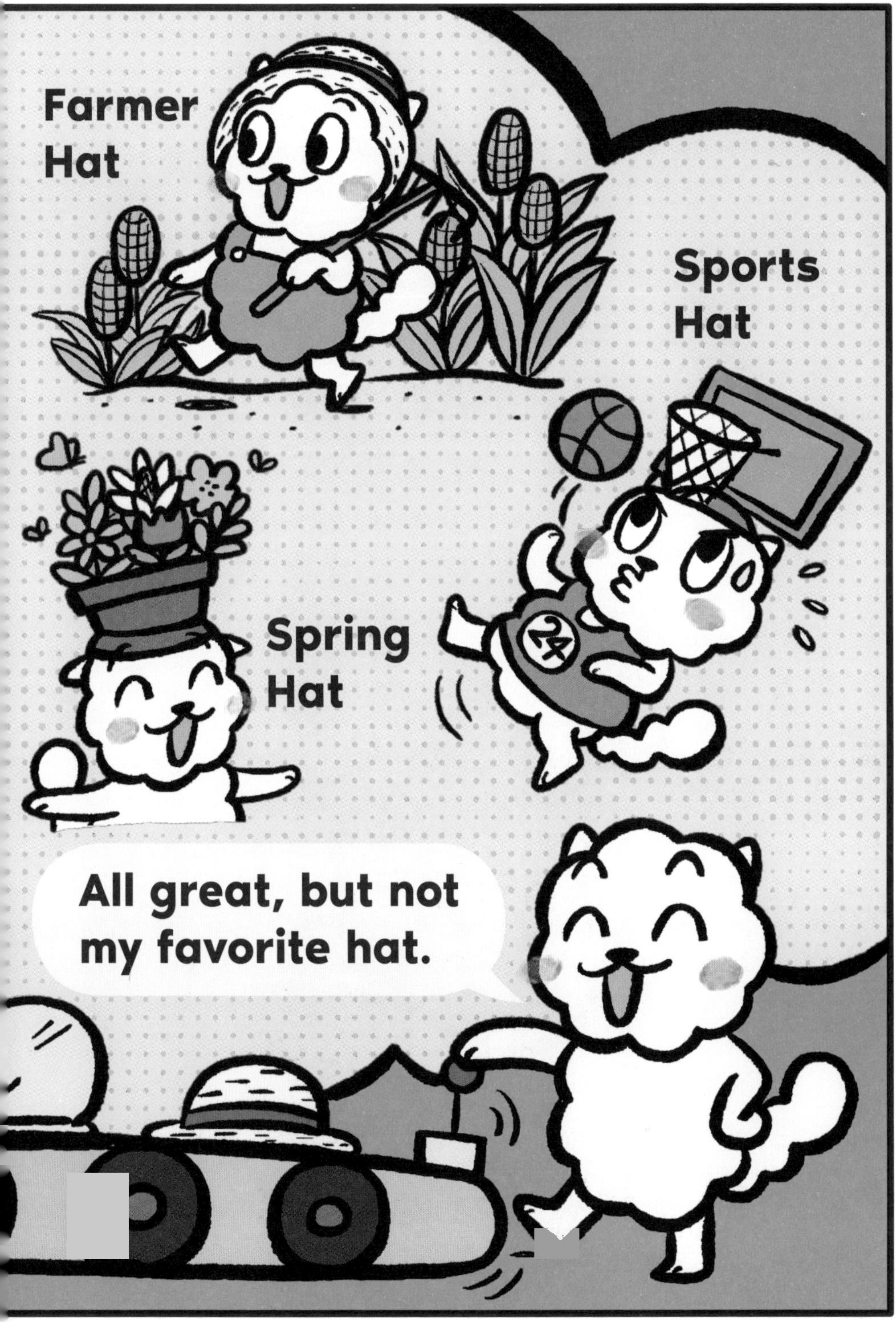
Farmer Hat
Sports Hat
Spring Hat
All great, but not my favorite hat.

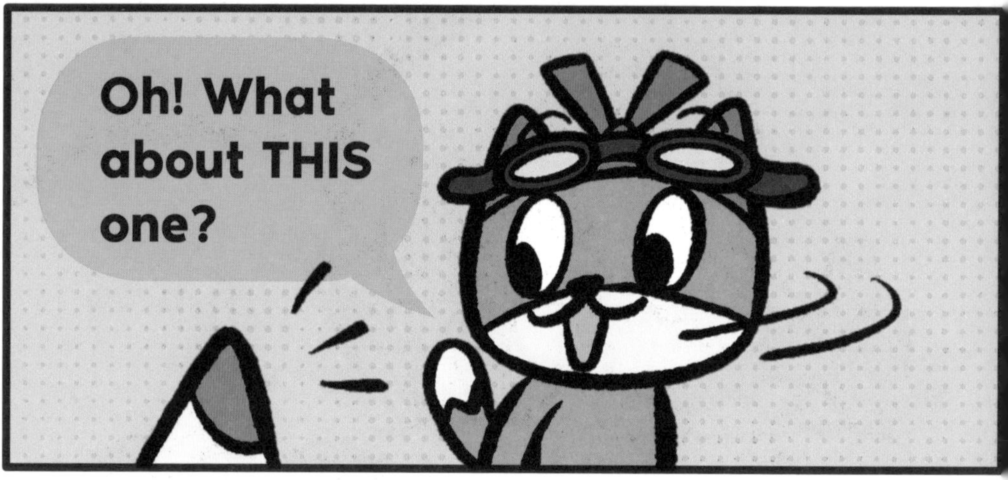
Oh! What about THIS one?

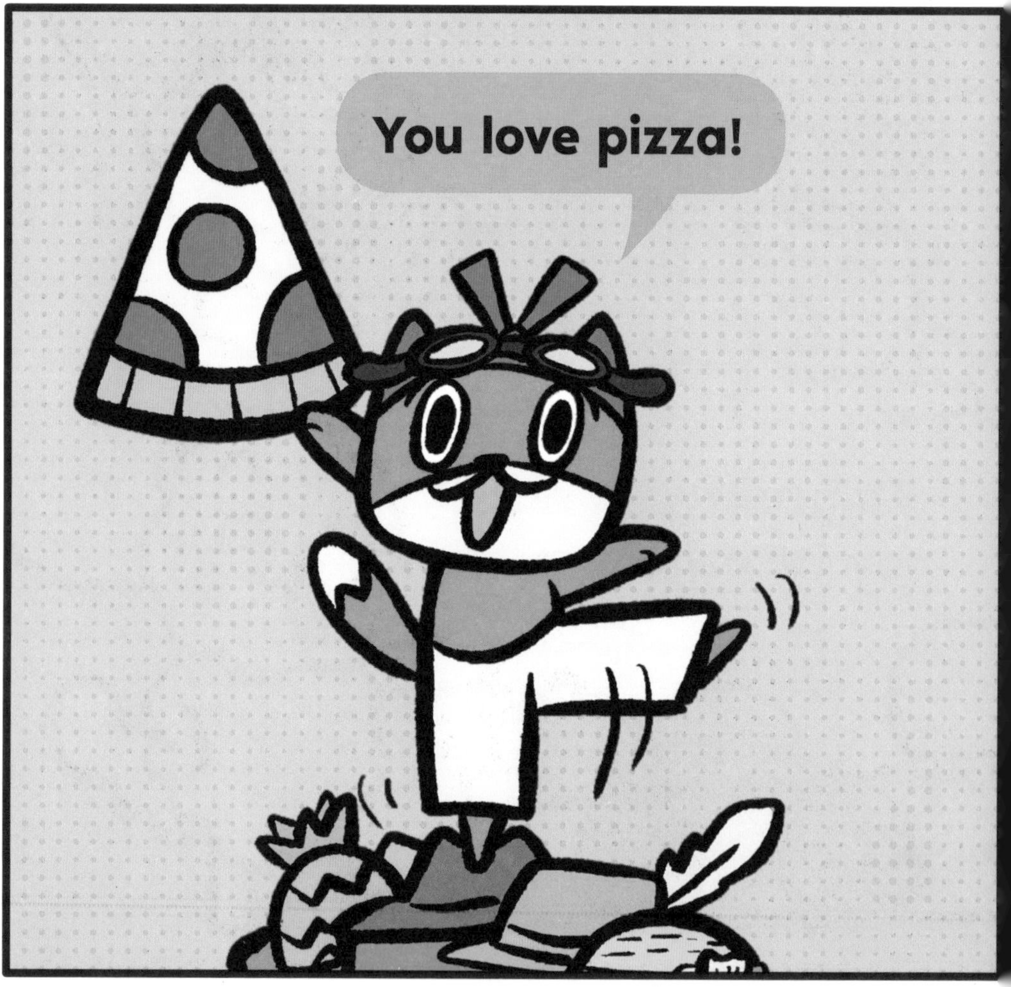
You love pizza!

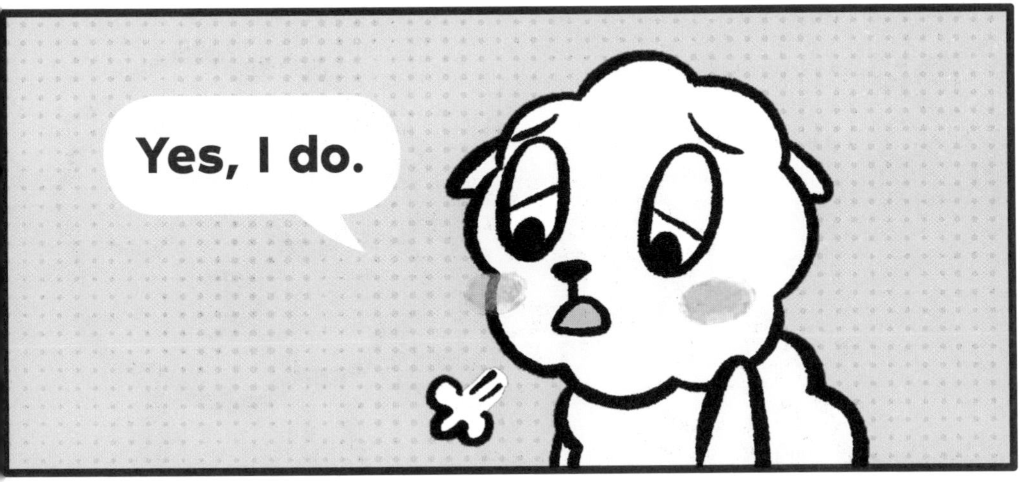
Yes, I do.

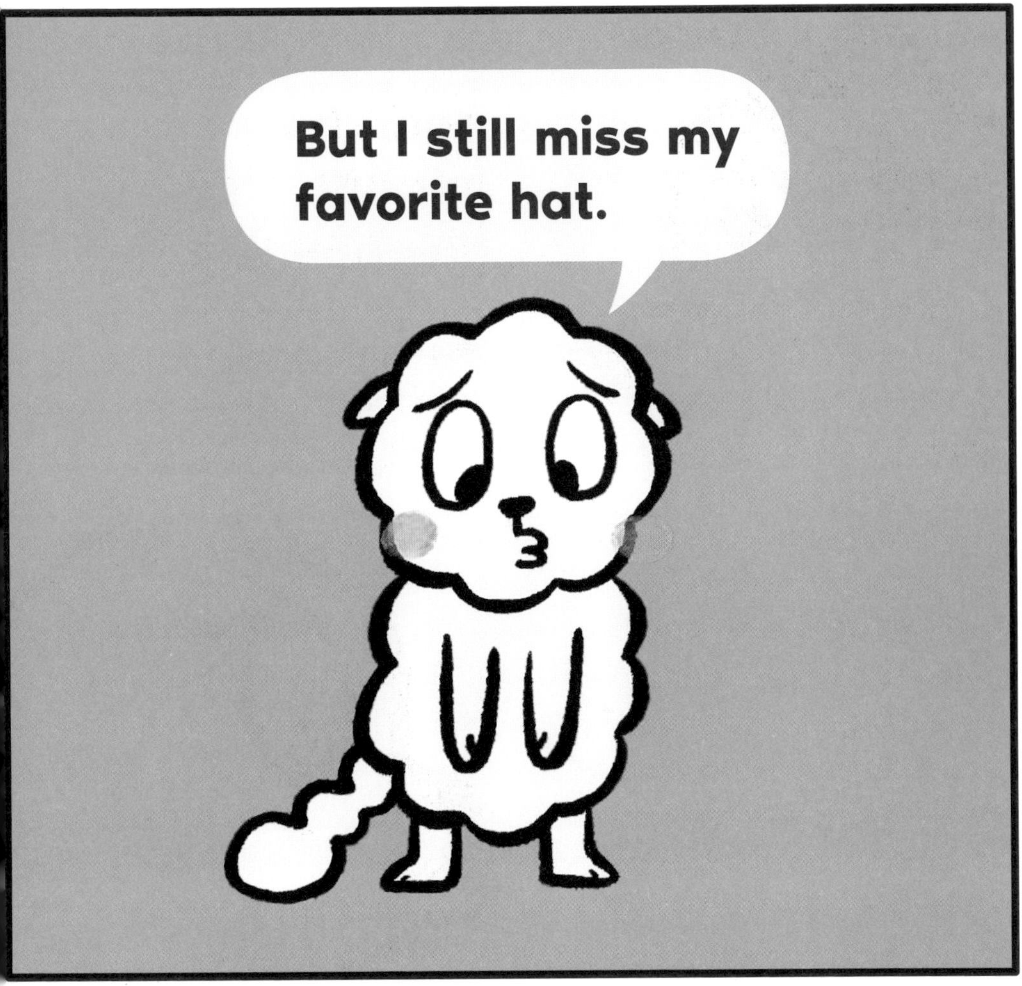
But I still miss my favorite hat.

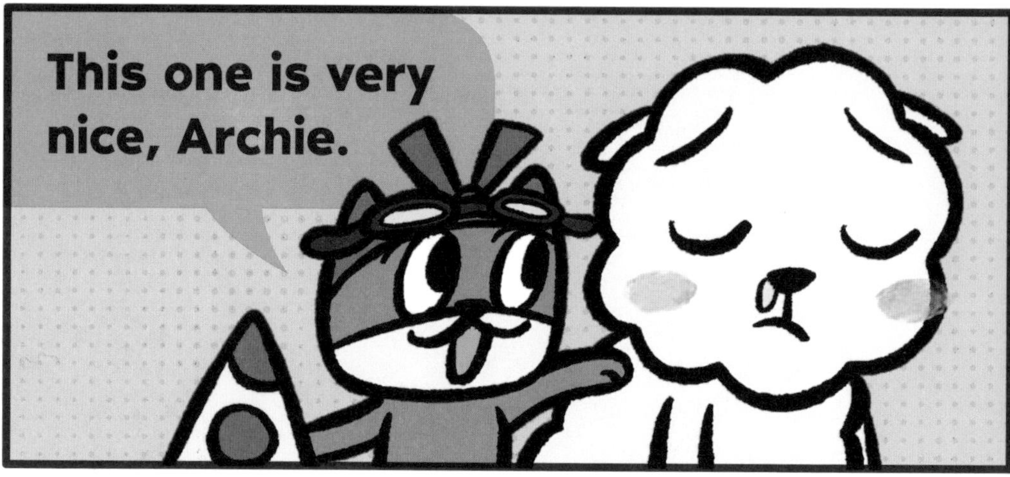
This one is very nice, Archie.

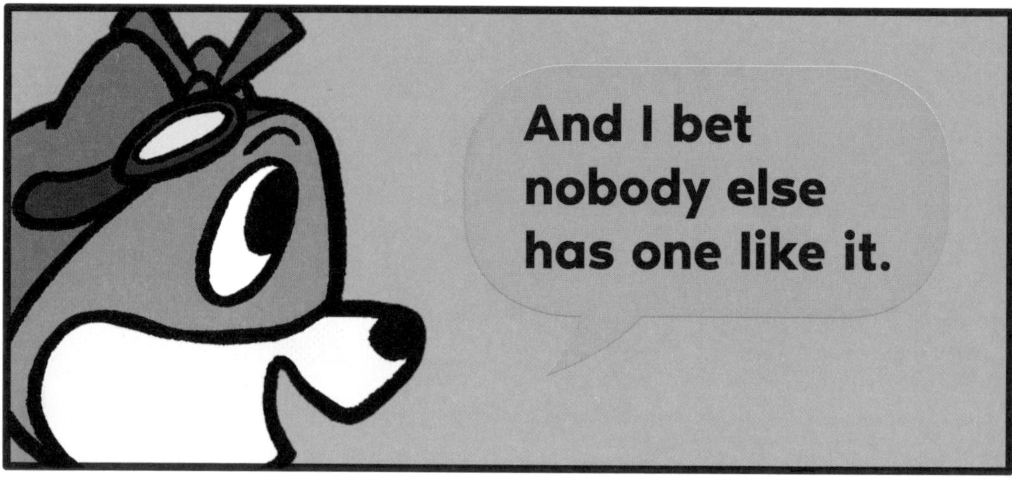
And I bet nobody else has one like it.

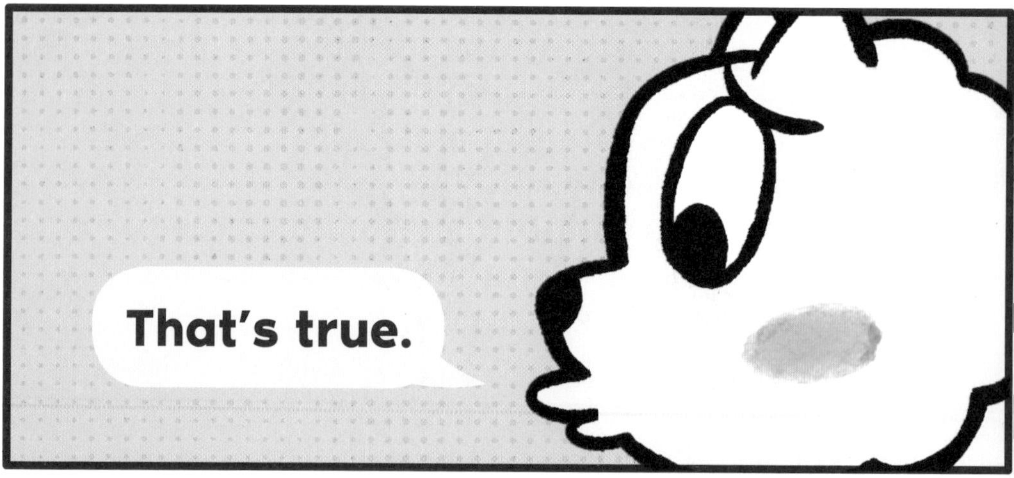
That's true.

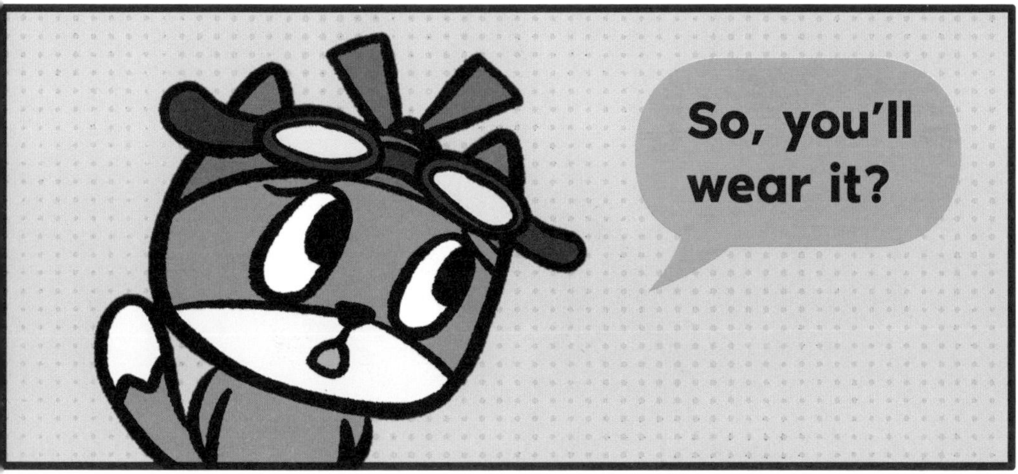
So, you'll wear it?

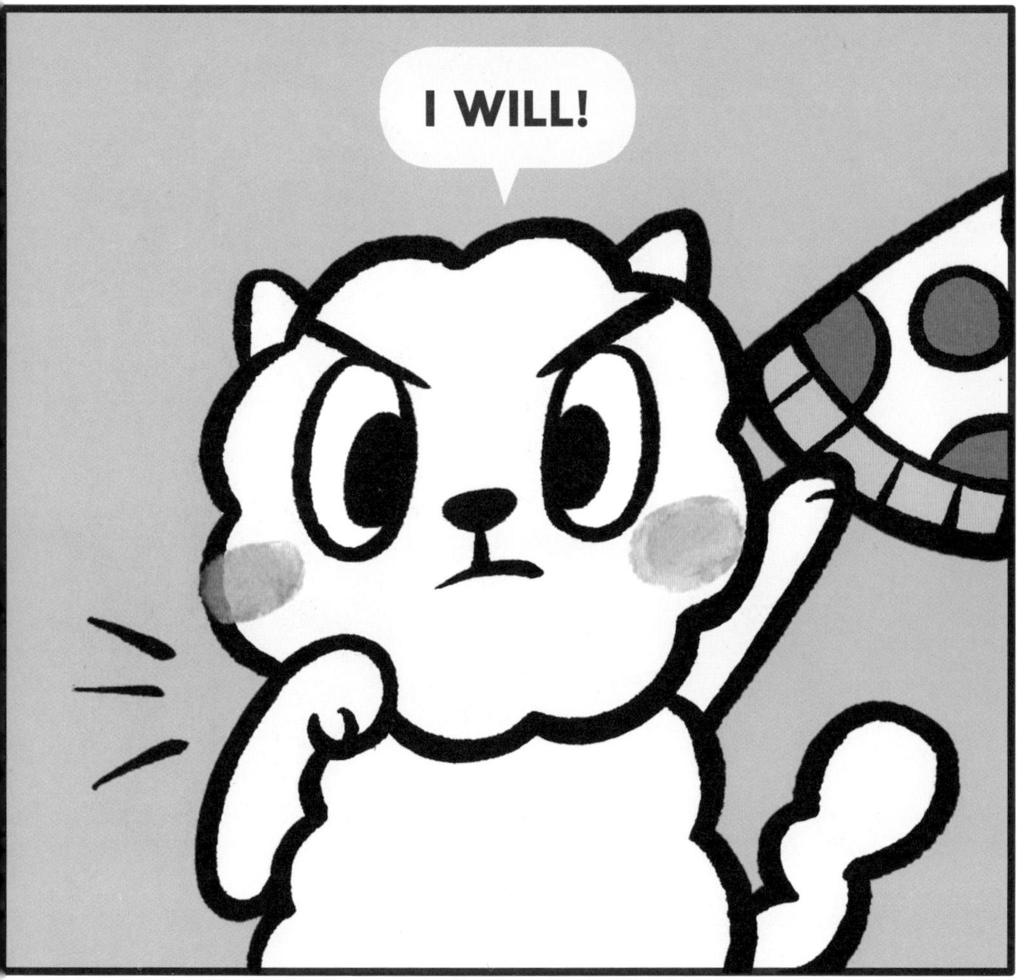
I WILL!

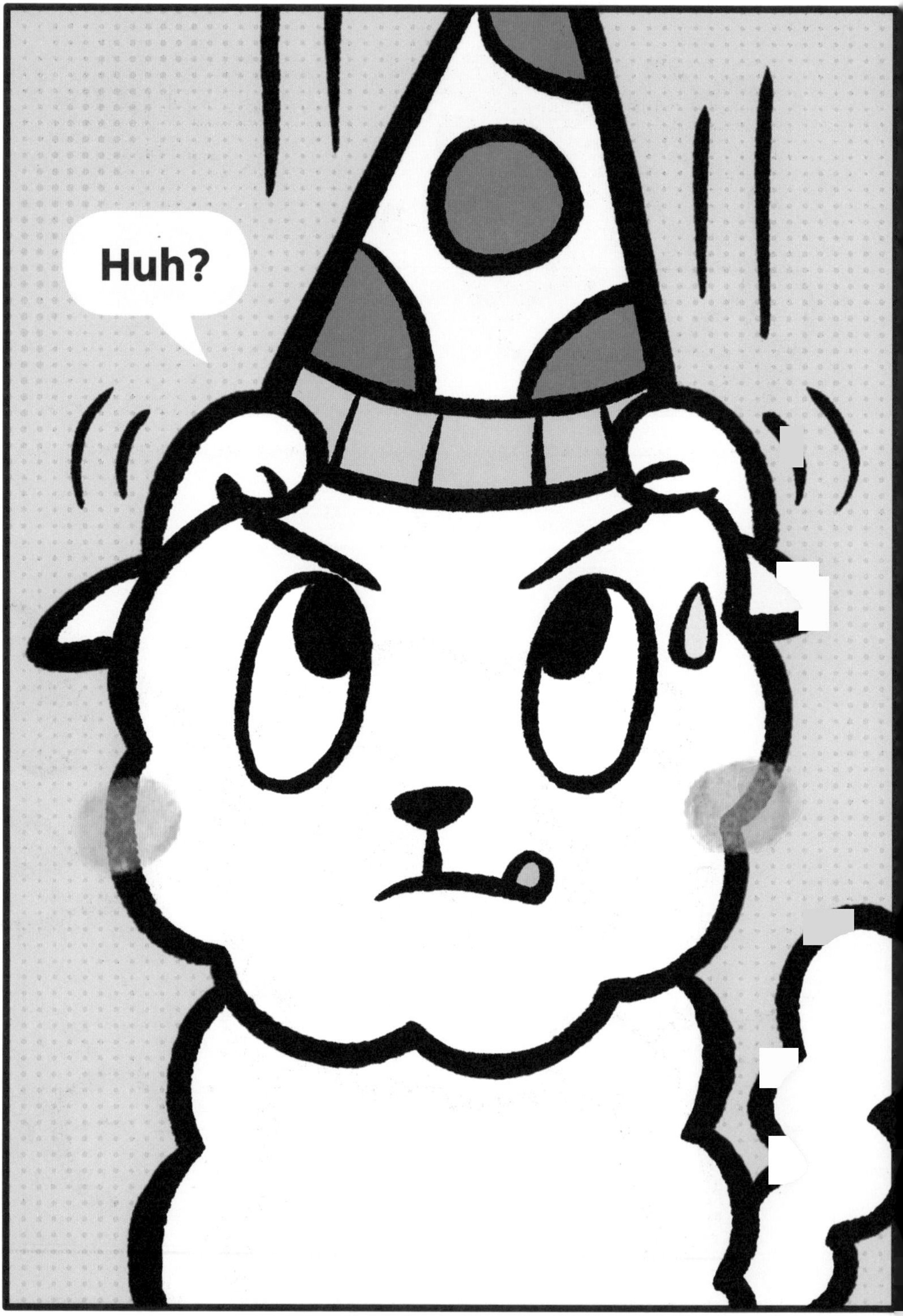
Huh?

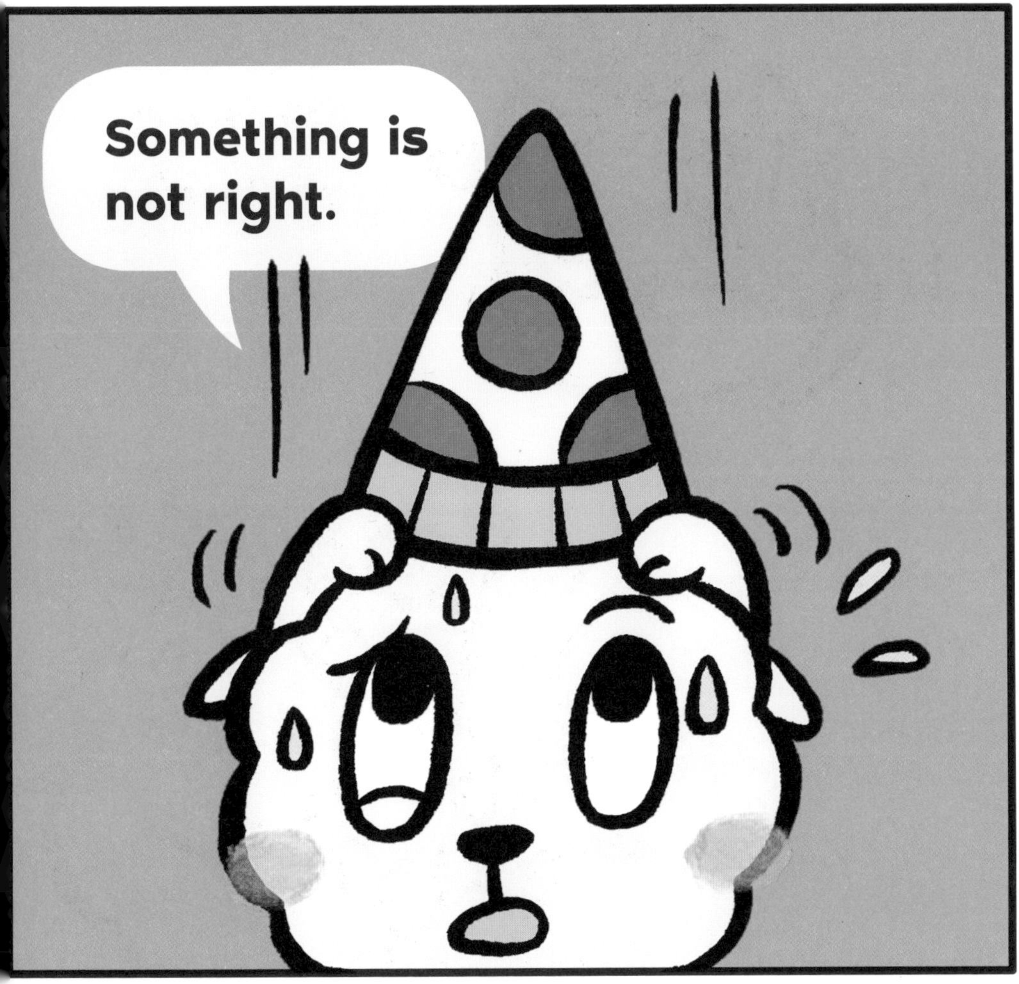
Something is not right.

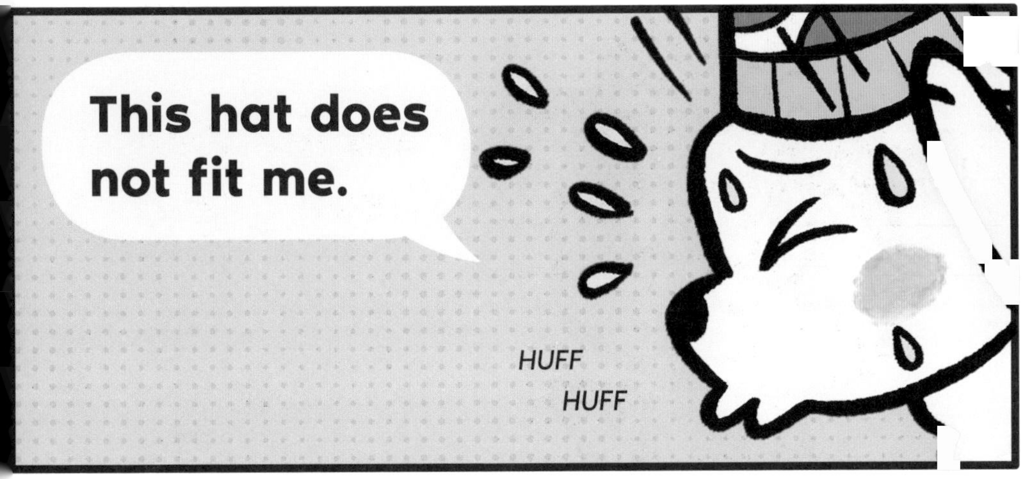
This hat does not fit me.
HUFF
HUFF

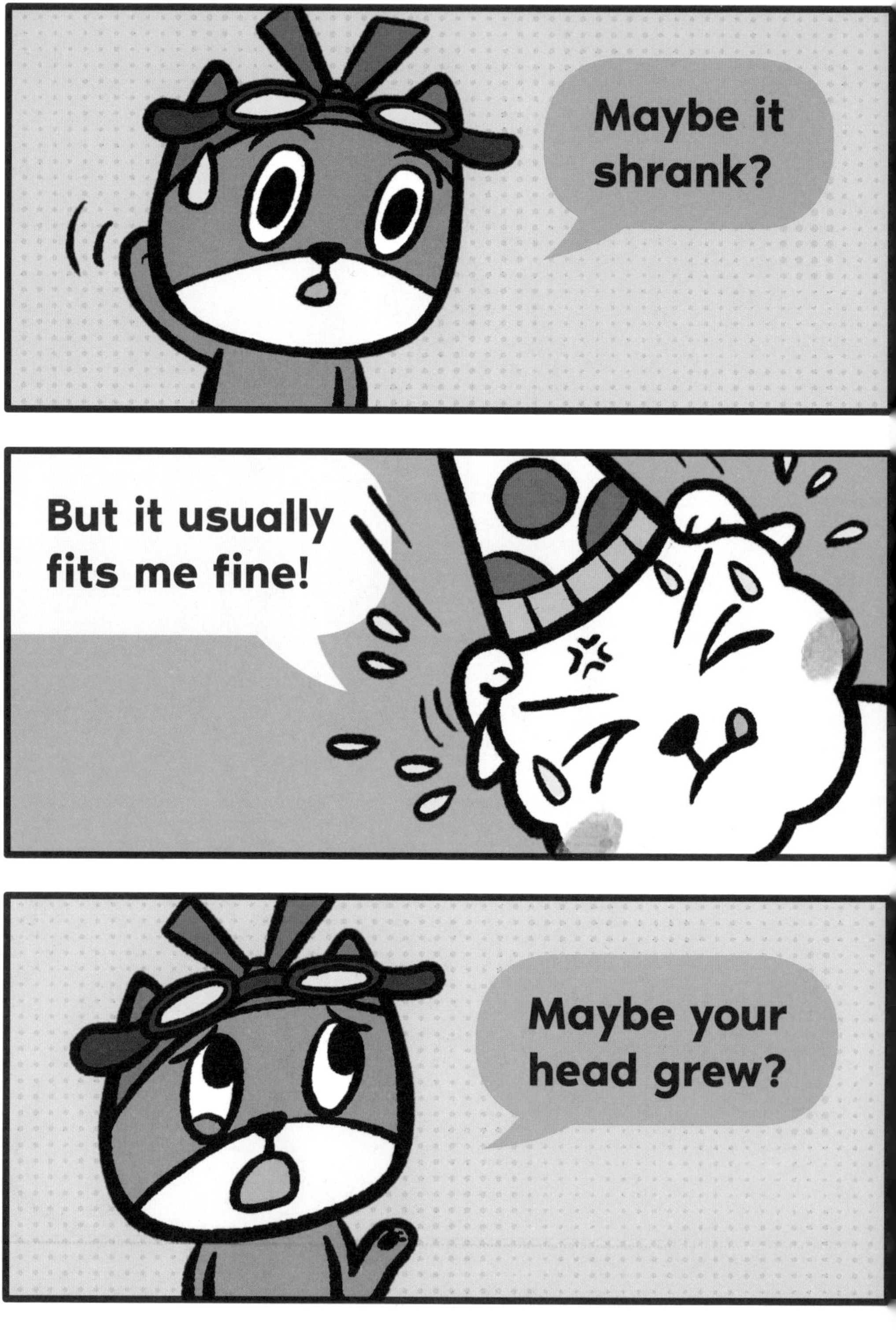
Maybe it shrank?
But it usually fits me fine!
Maybe your head grew?

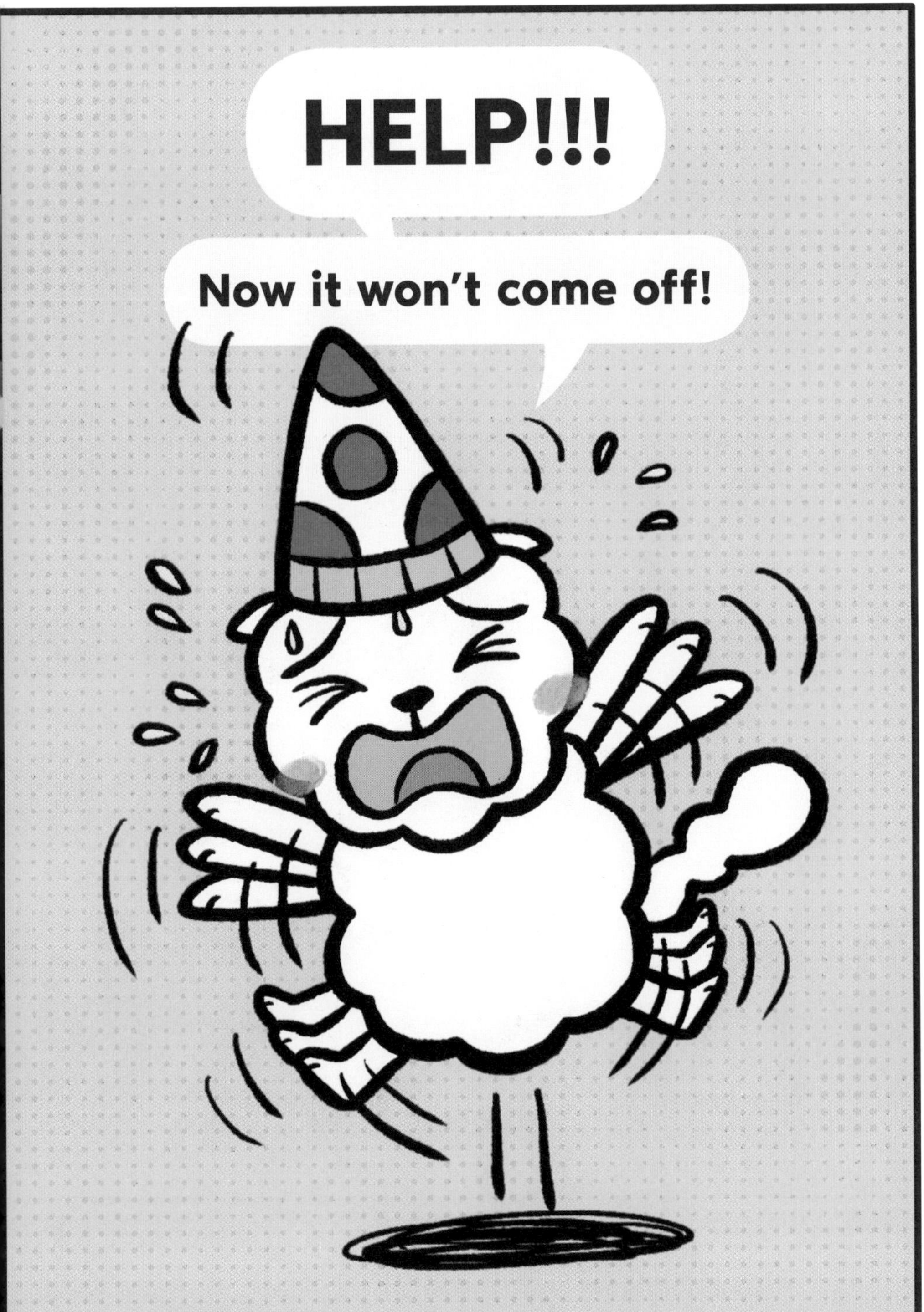
HELP!!!
Now it won't come off!

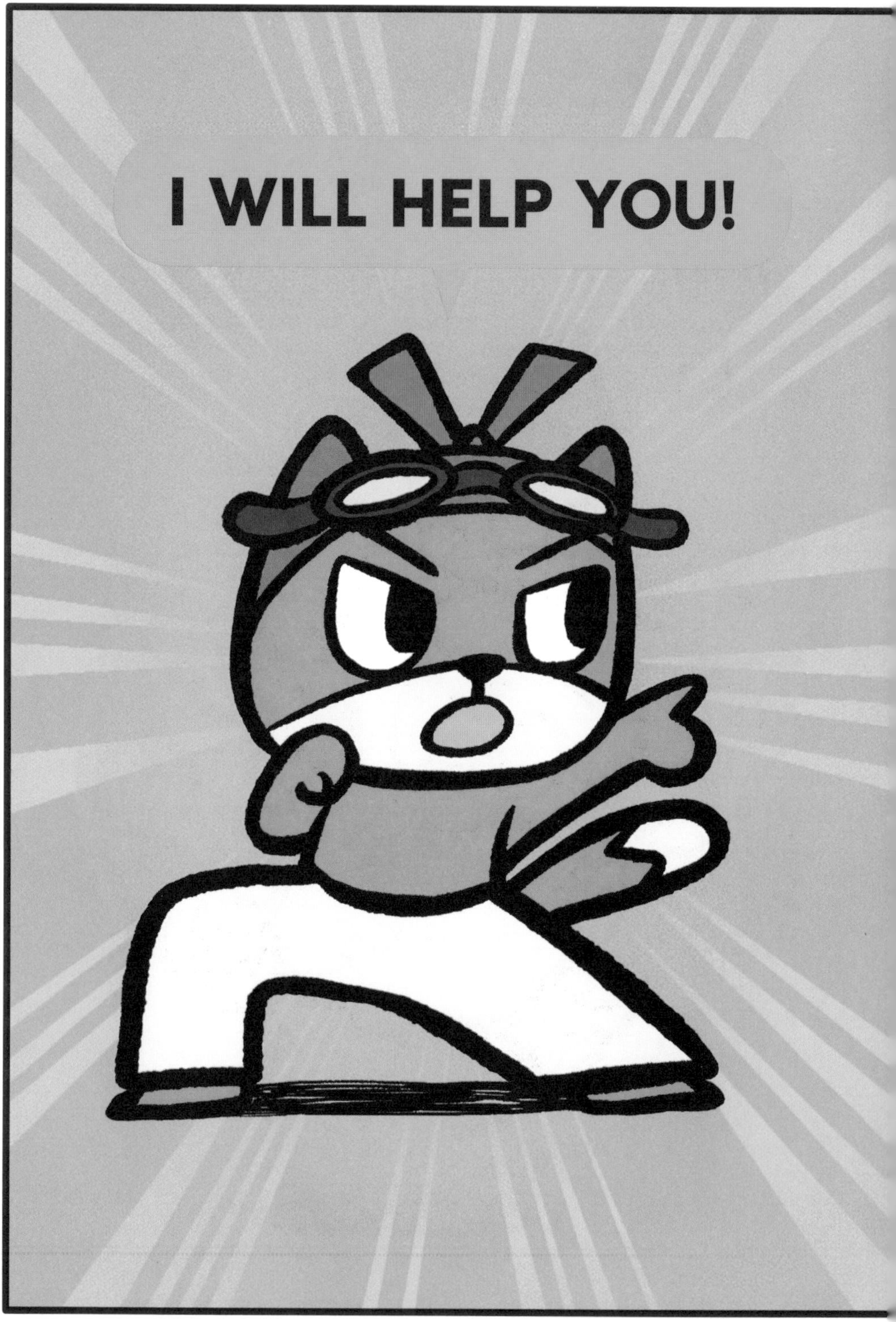
I WILL HELP YOU!

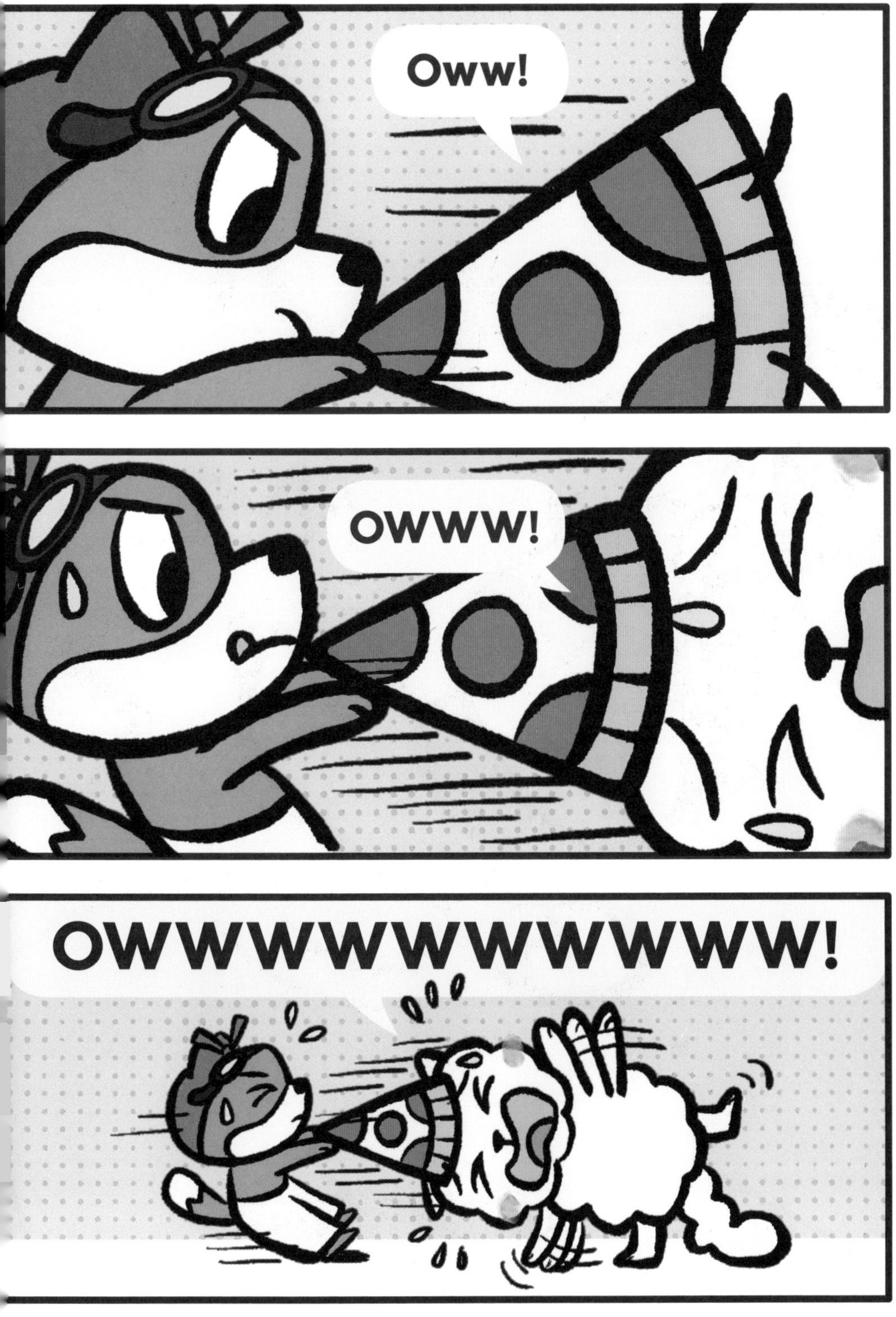
Oww!
OWWW!
OWWWWWWWWWWW!

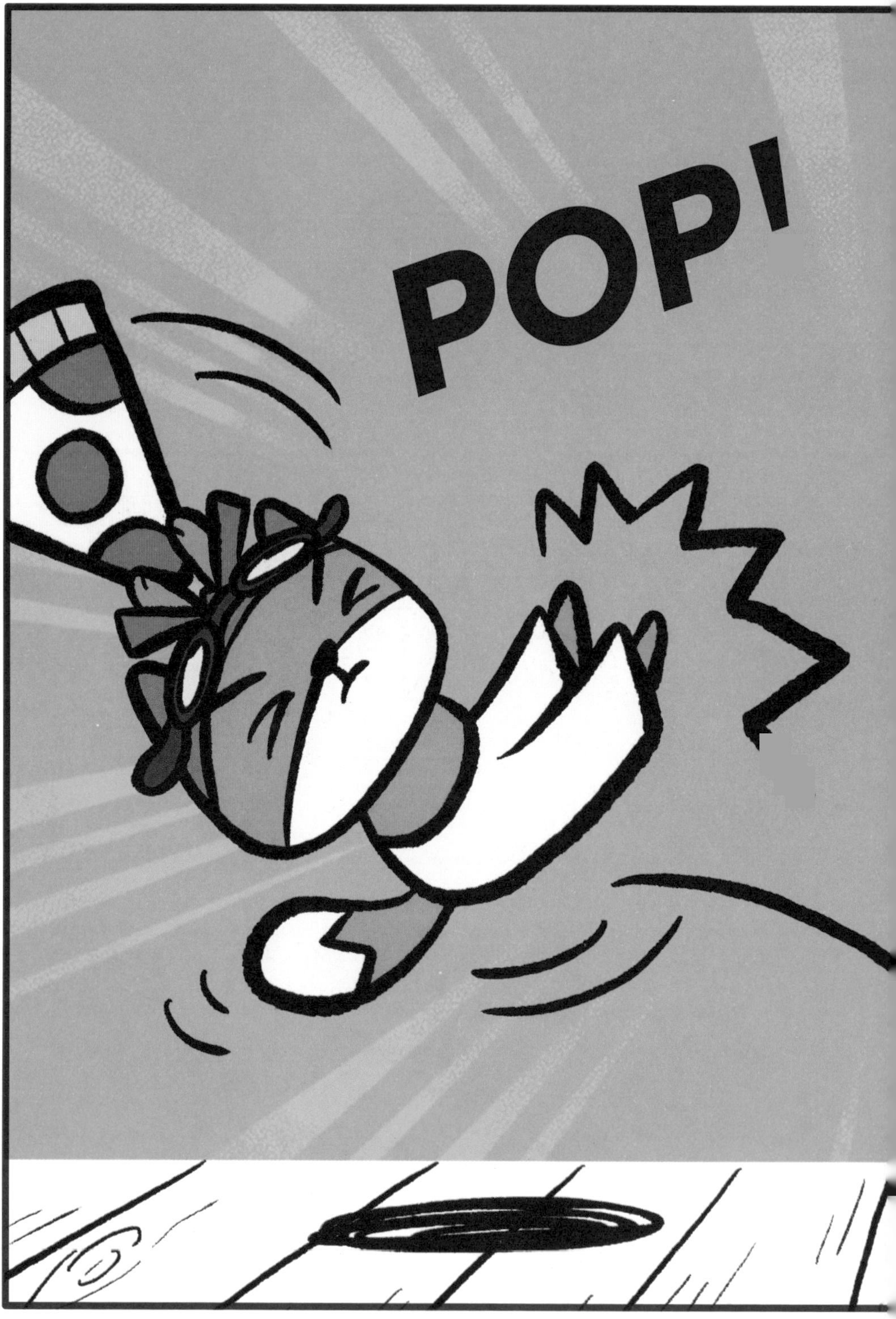
POP!

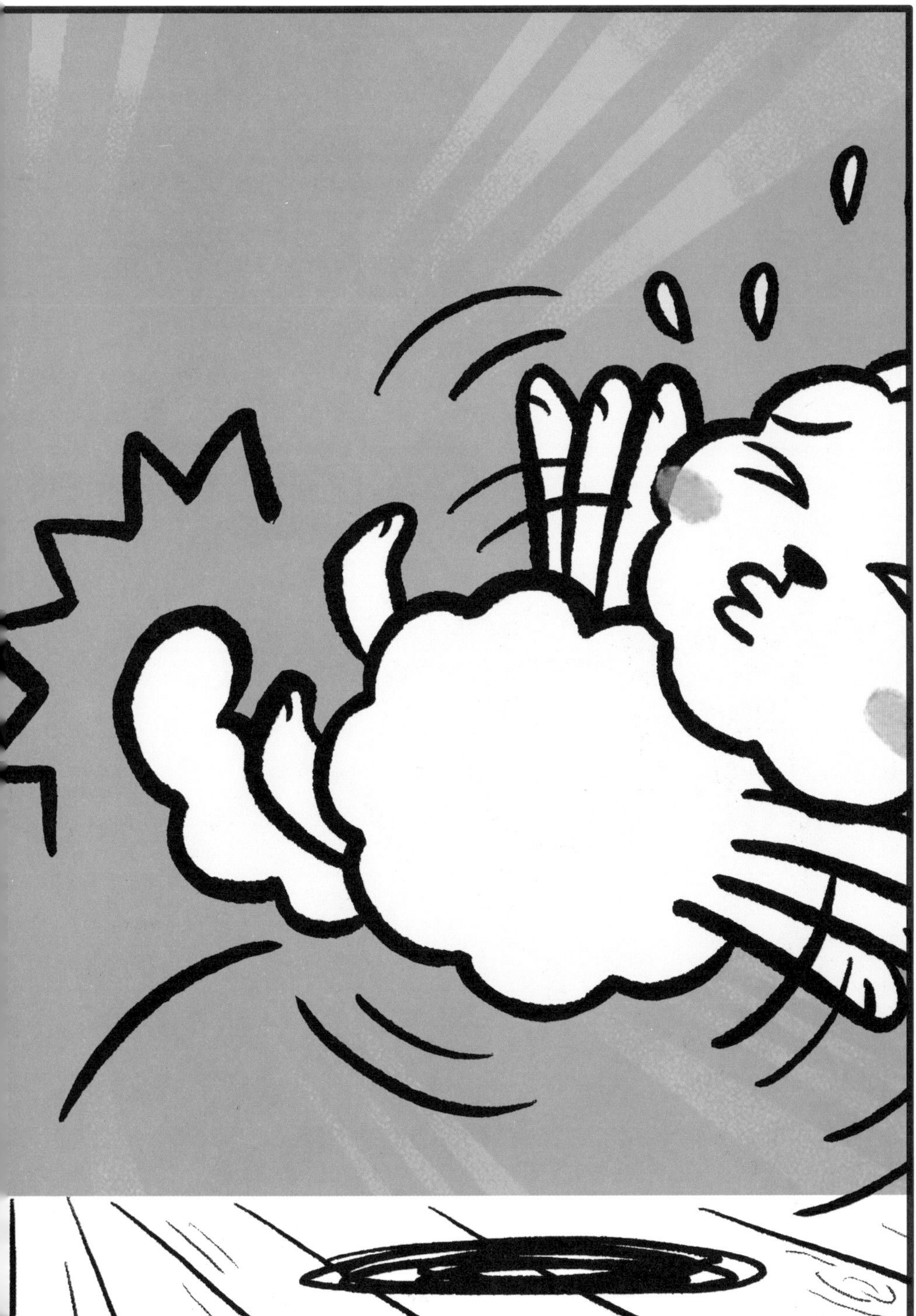

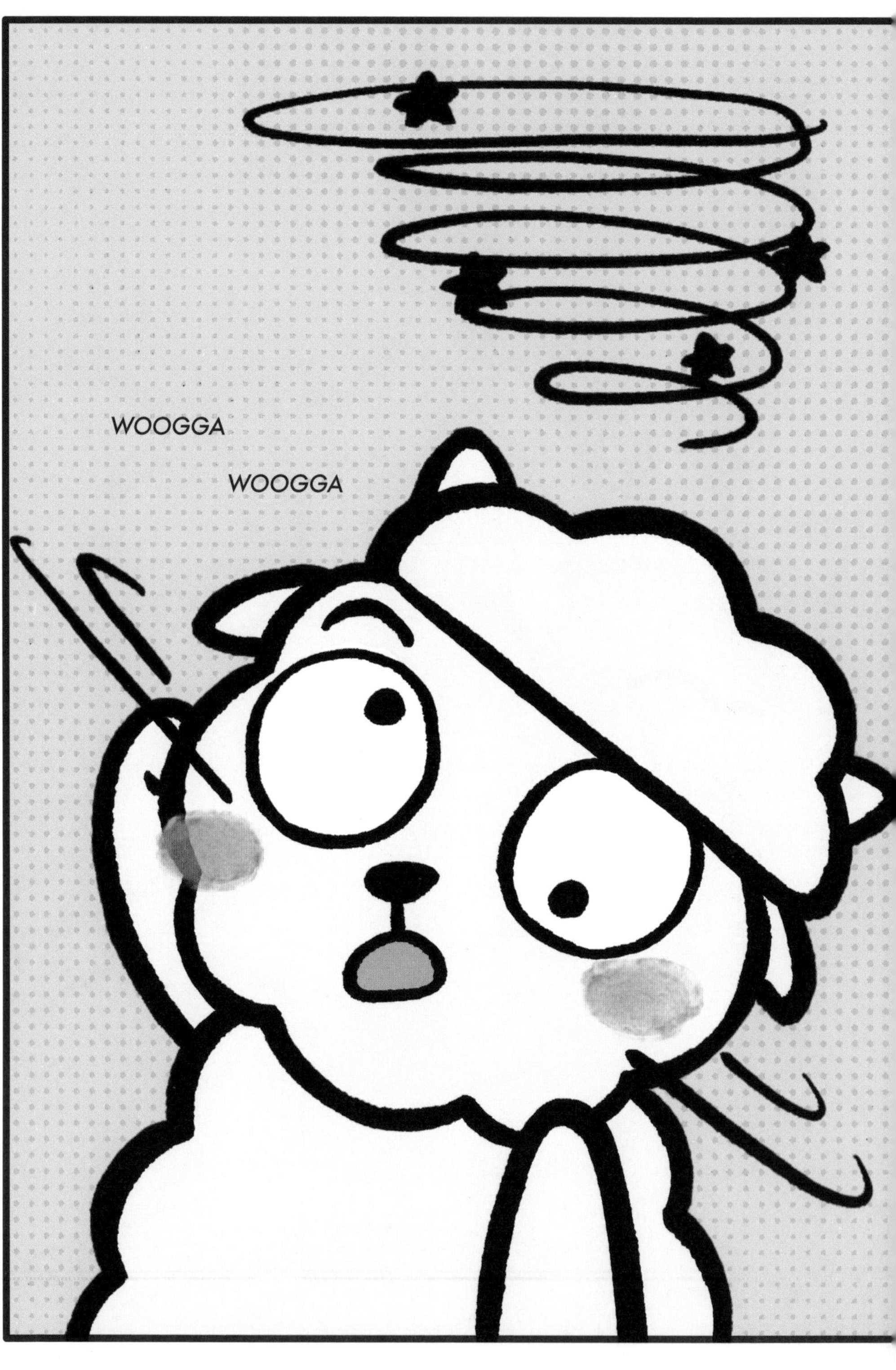
WOOGGA
WOOGGA

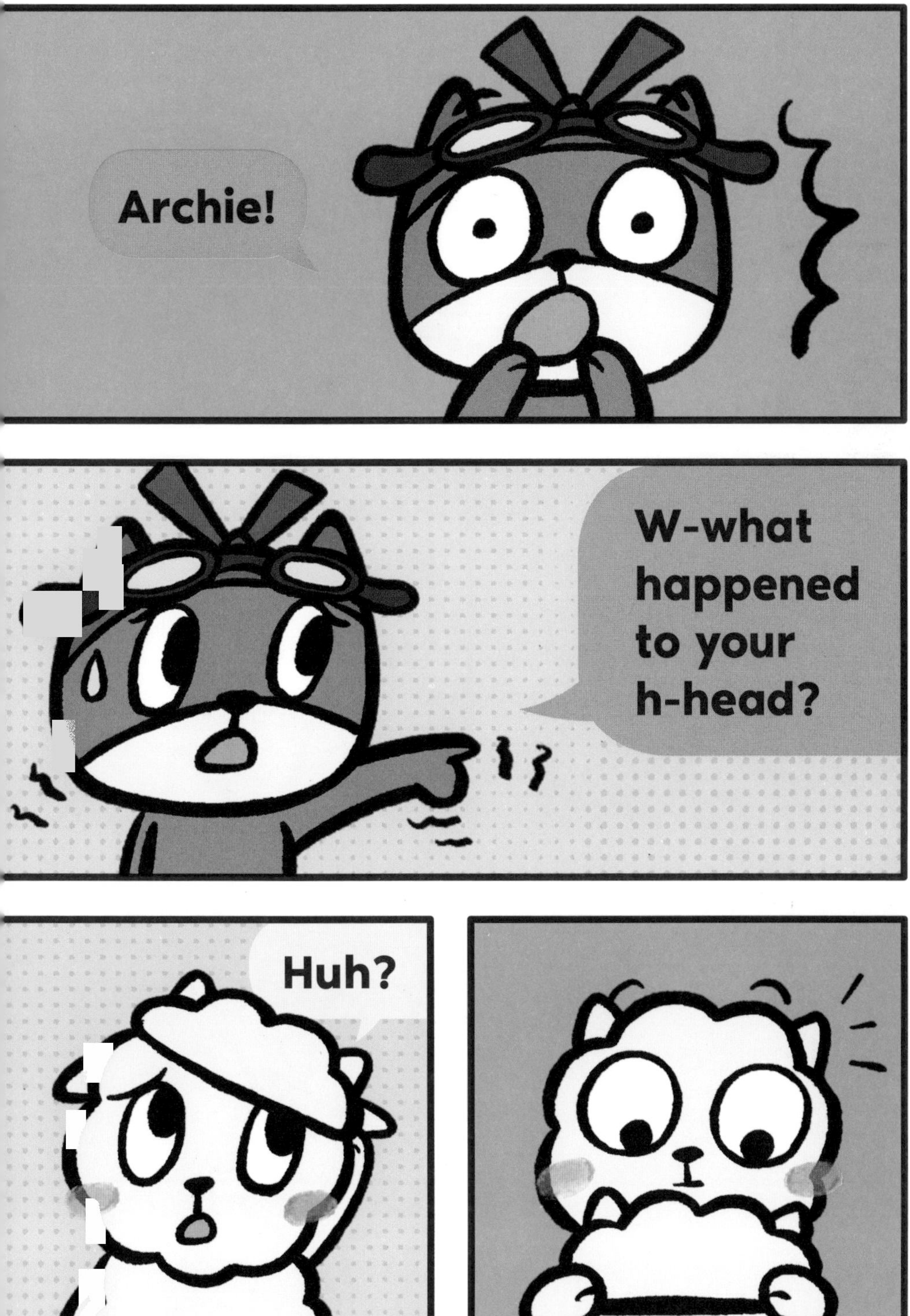
Archie!
W-what happened to your h-head?
Huh?

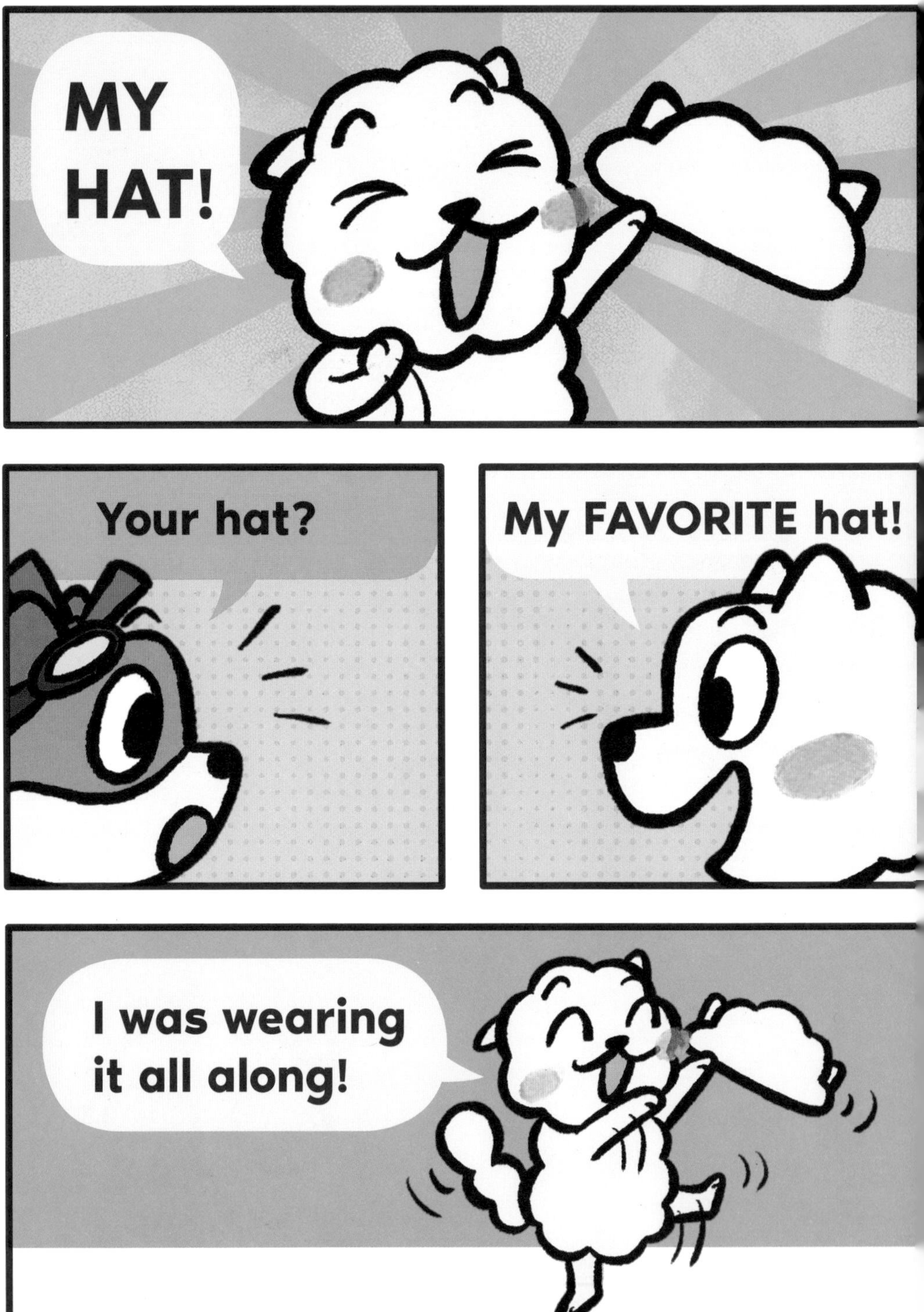
MY HAT!
Your hat?
My FAVORITE hat!
I was wearing it all along!

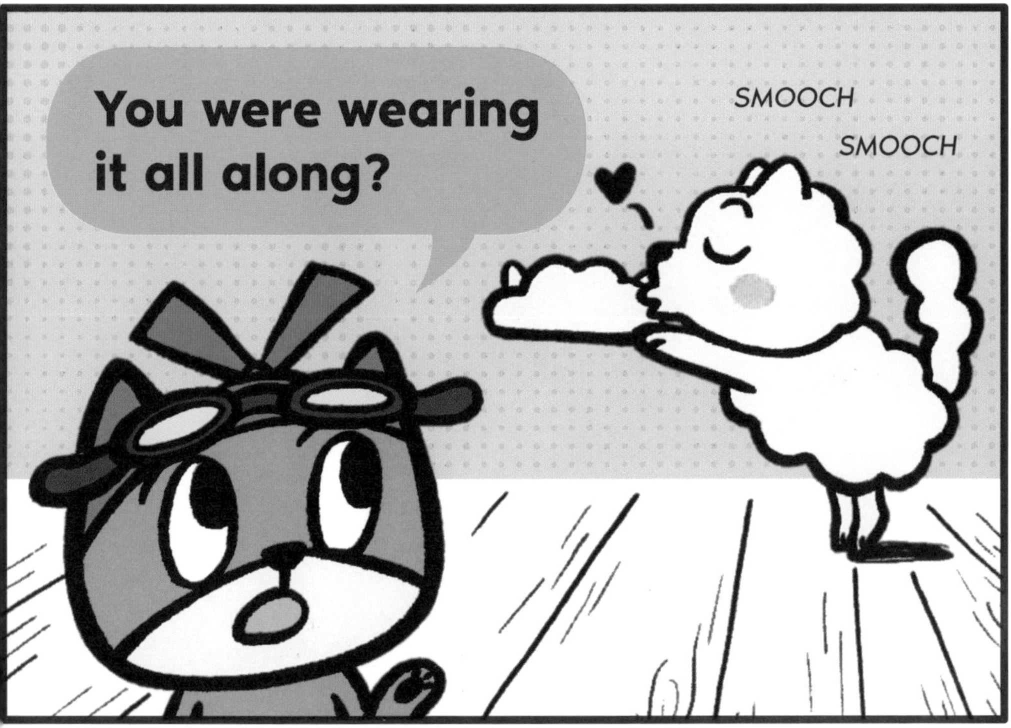
You were wearing it all along?
SMOOCH
SMOOCH

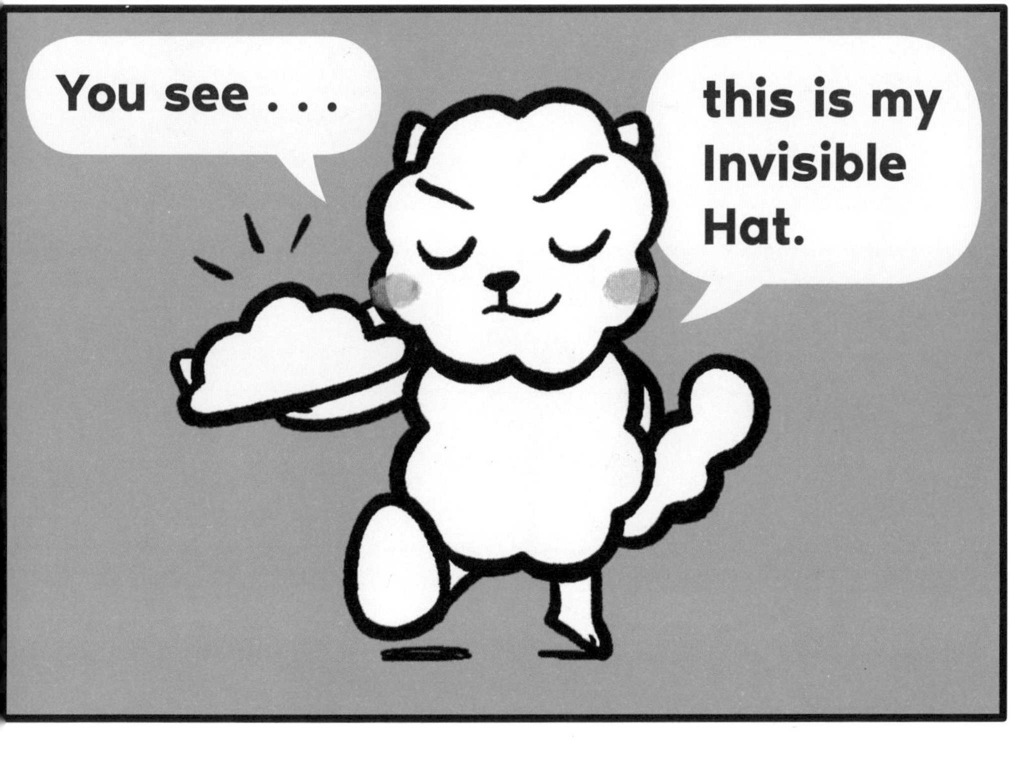
You see . . .
this is my Invisible Hat.

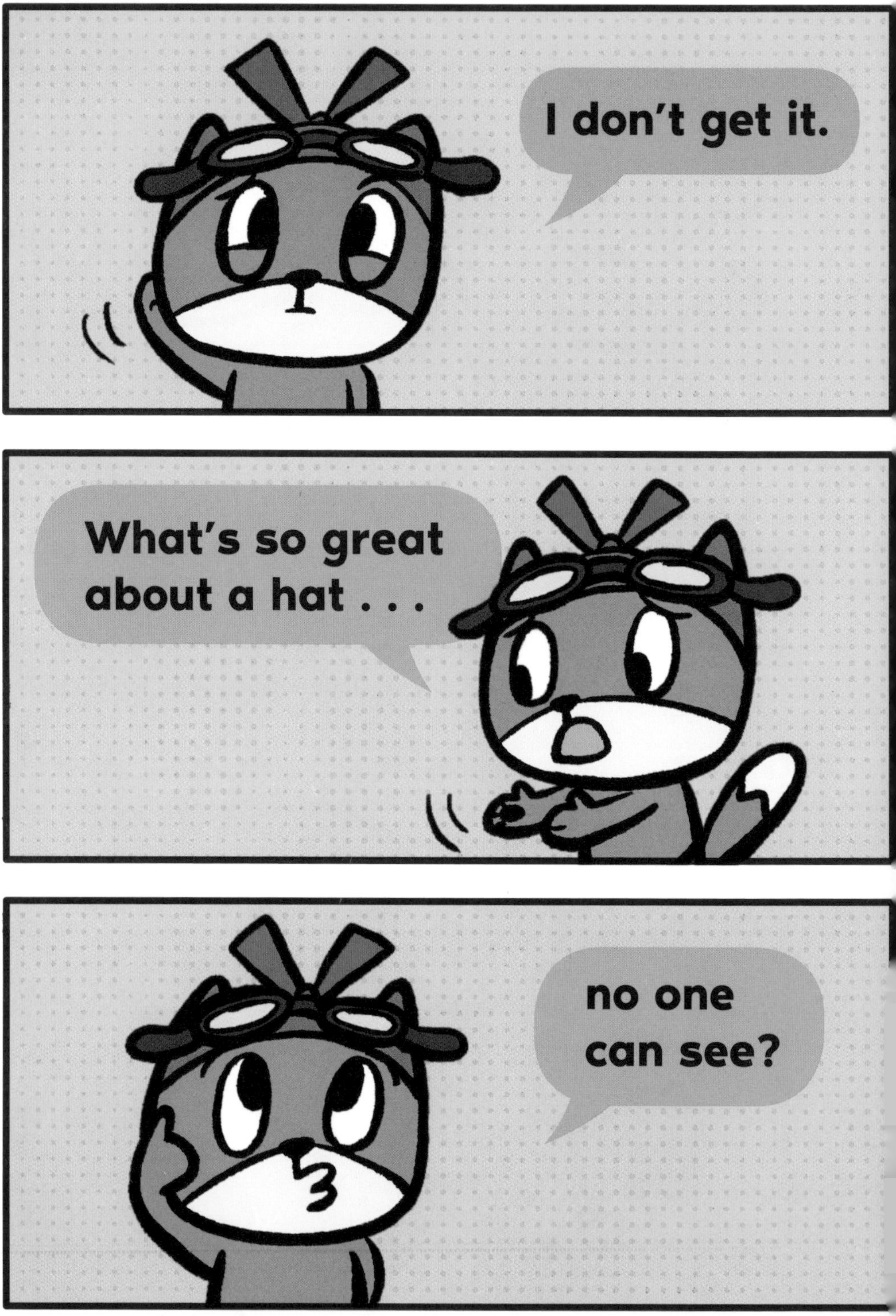
I don't get it.
What's so great about a hat . . .
no one can see?

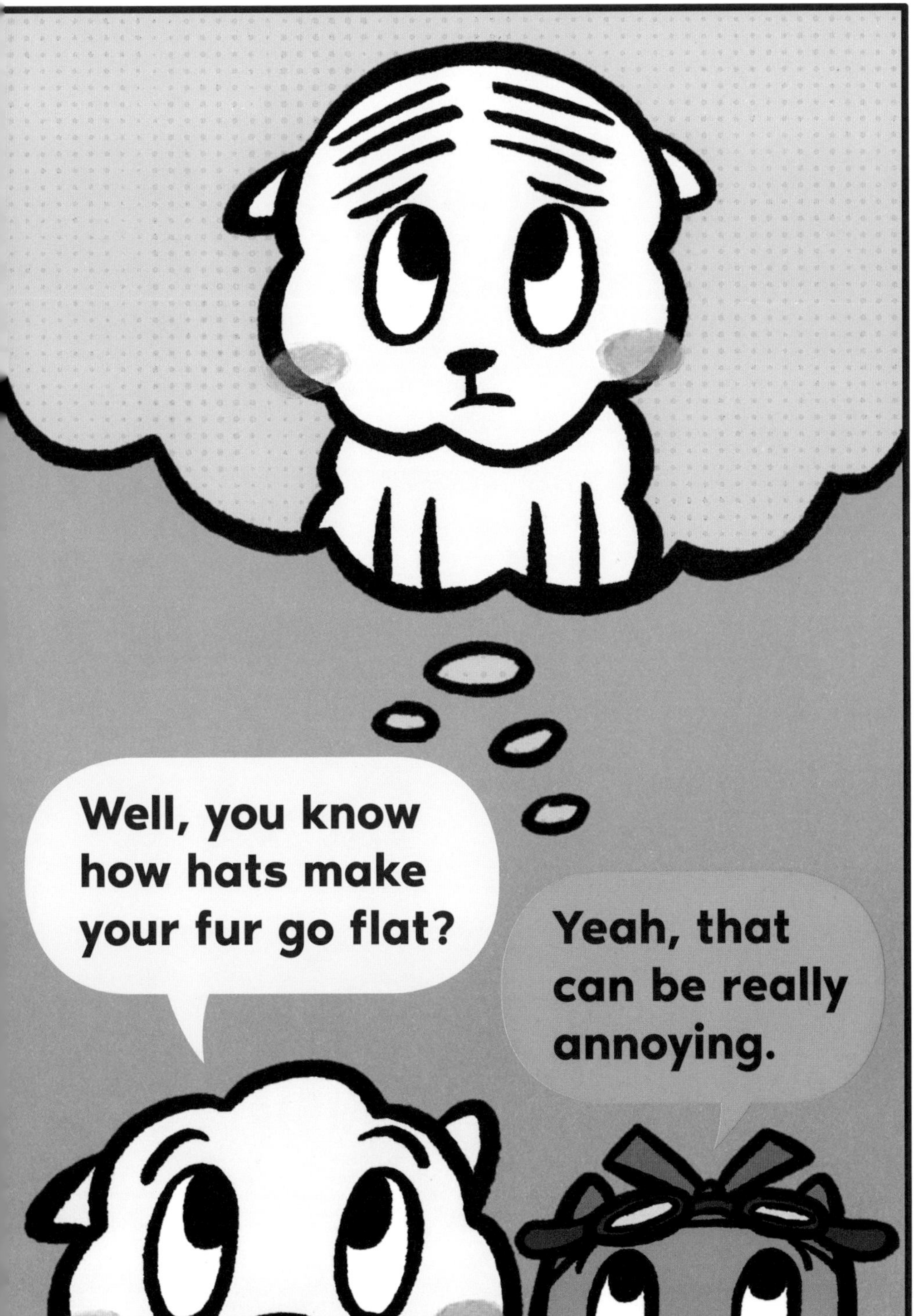
Well, you know how hats make your fur go flat?
Yeah, that can be really annoying.

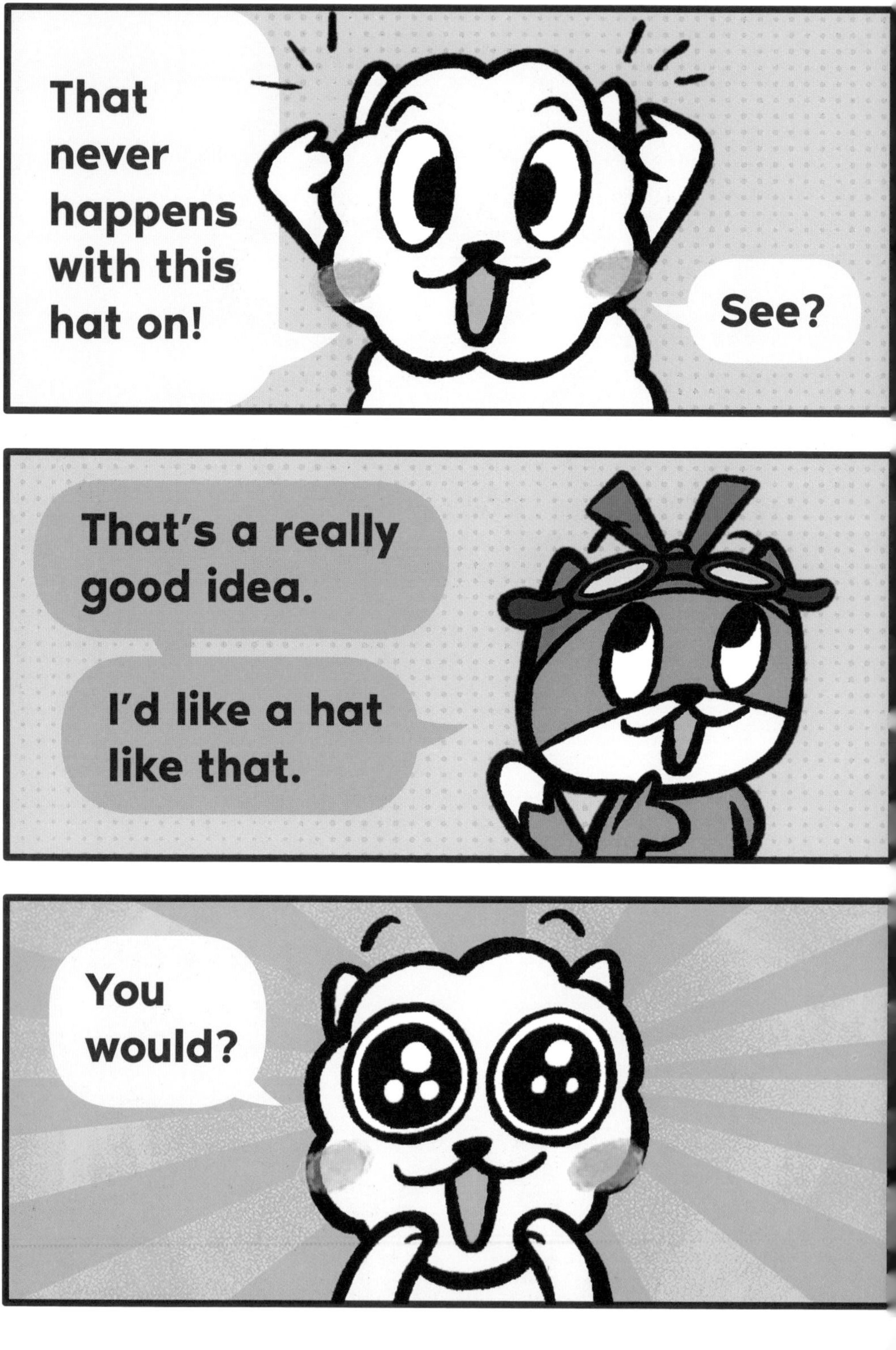
That never happens with this hat on!
See?
That's a really good idea.
I'd like a hat like that.
You would?

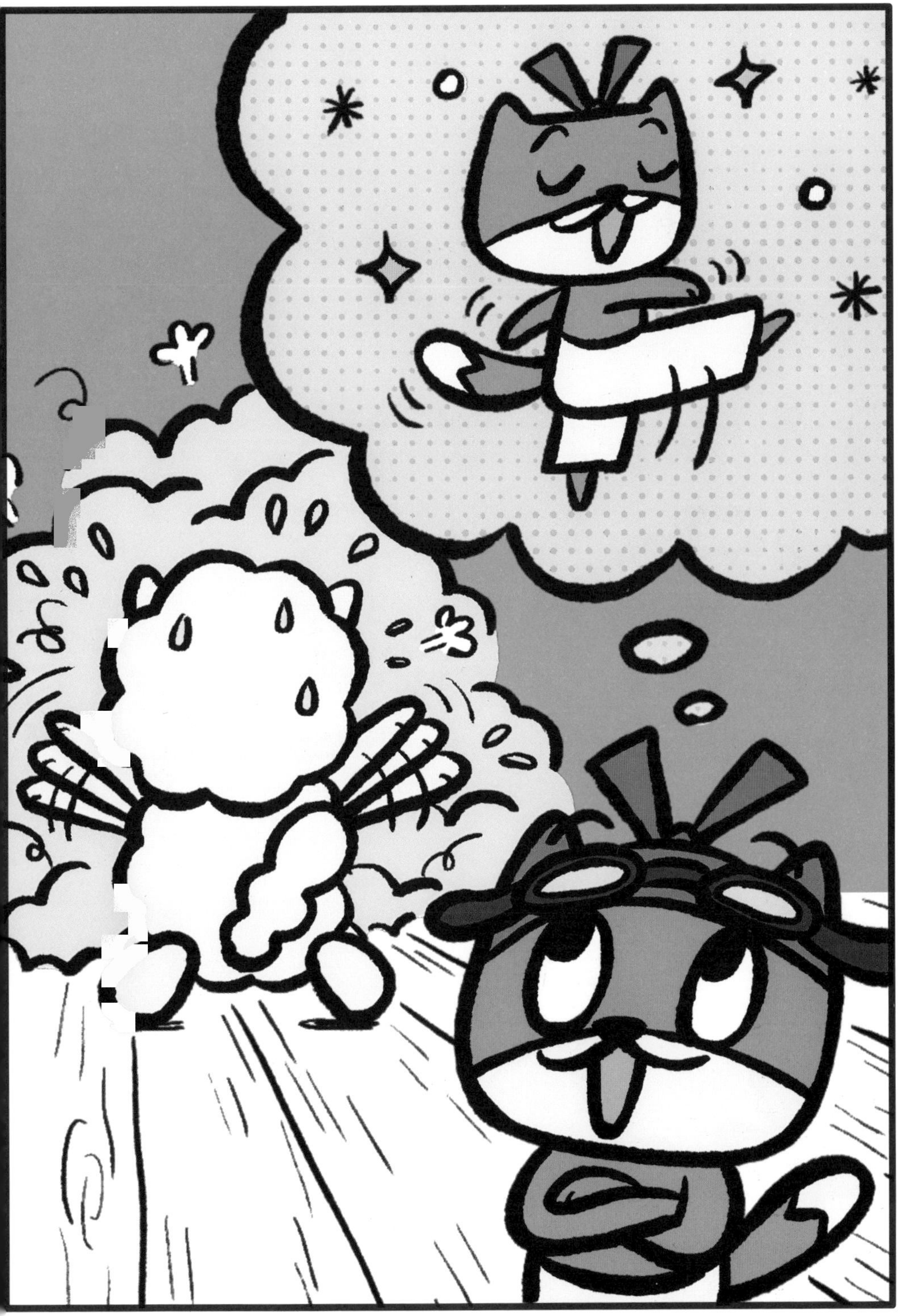

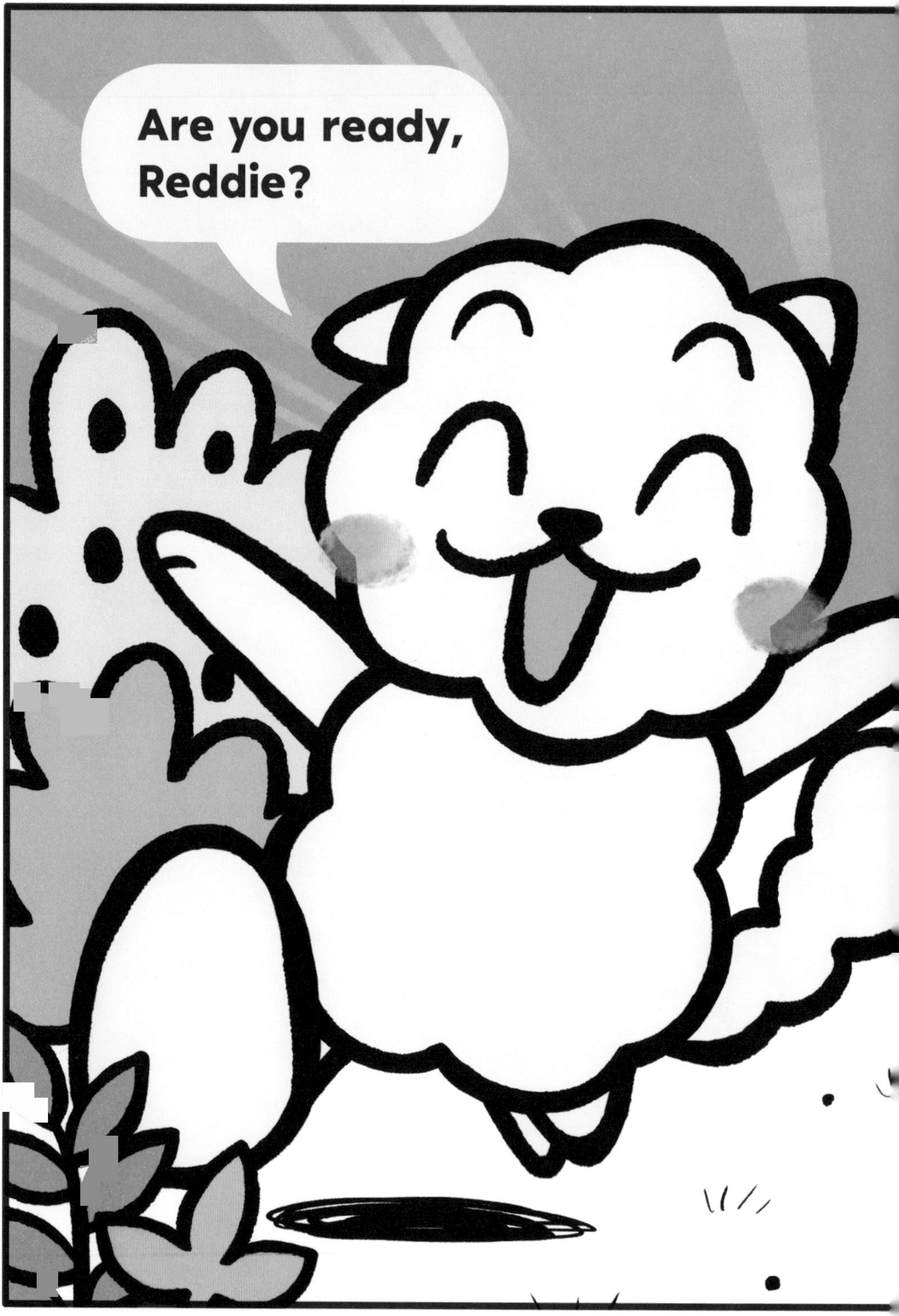
Are you ready, Reddie?

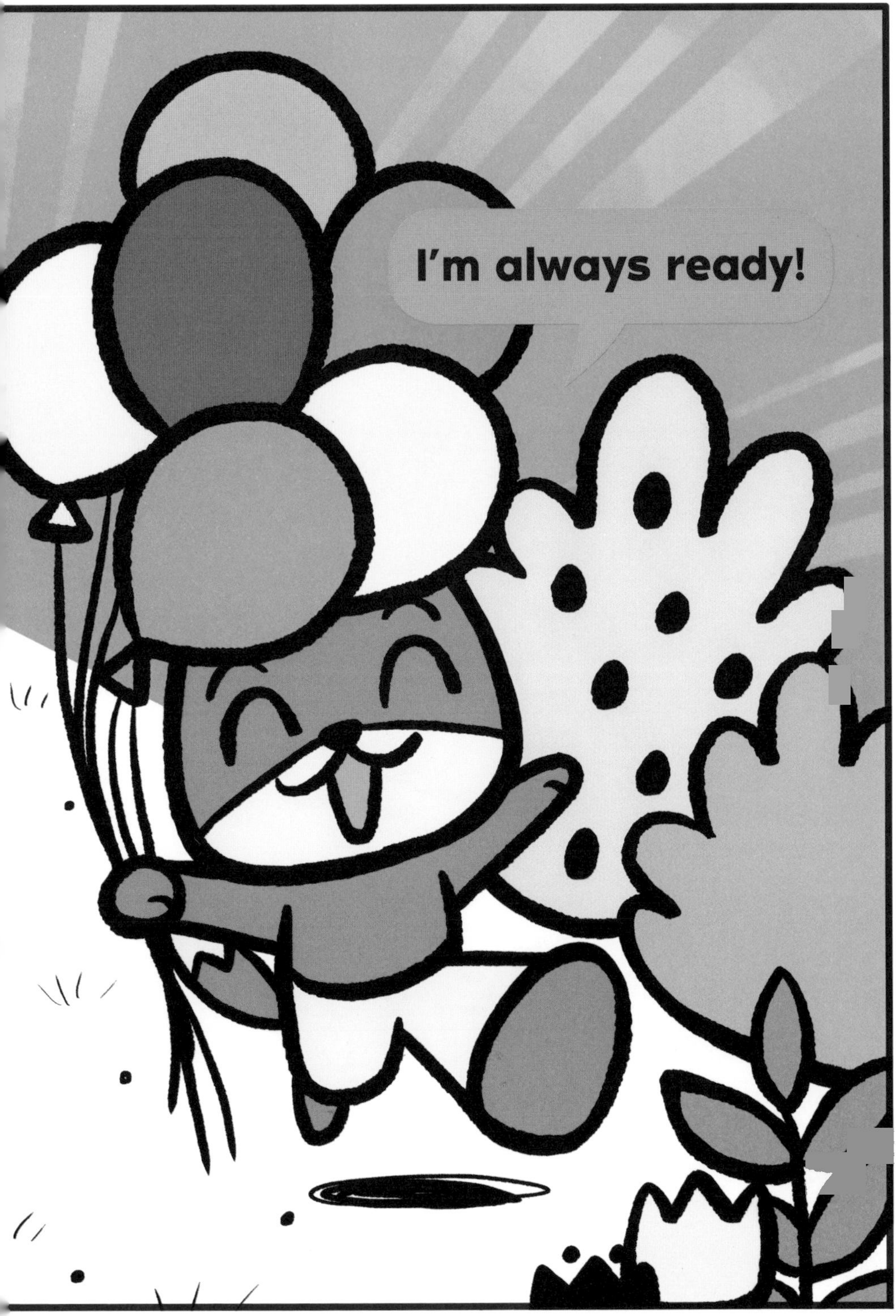
I'm always ready!

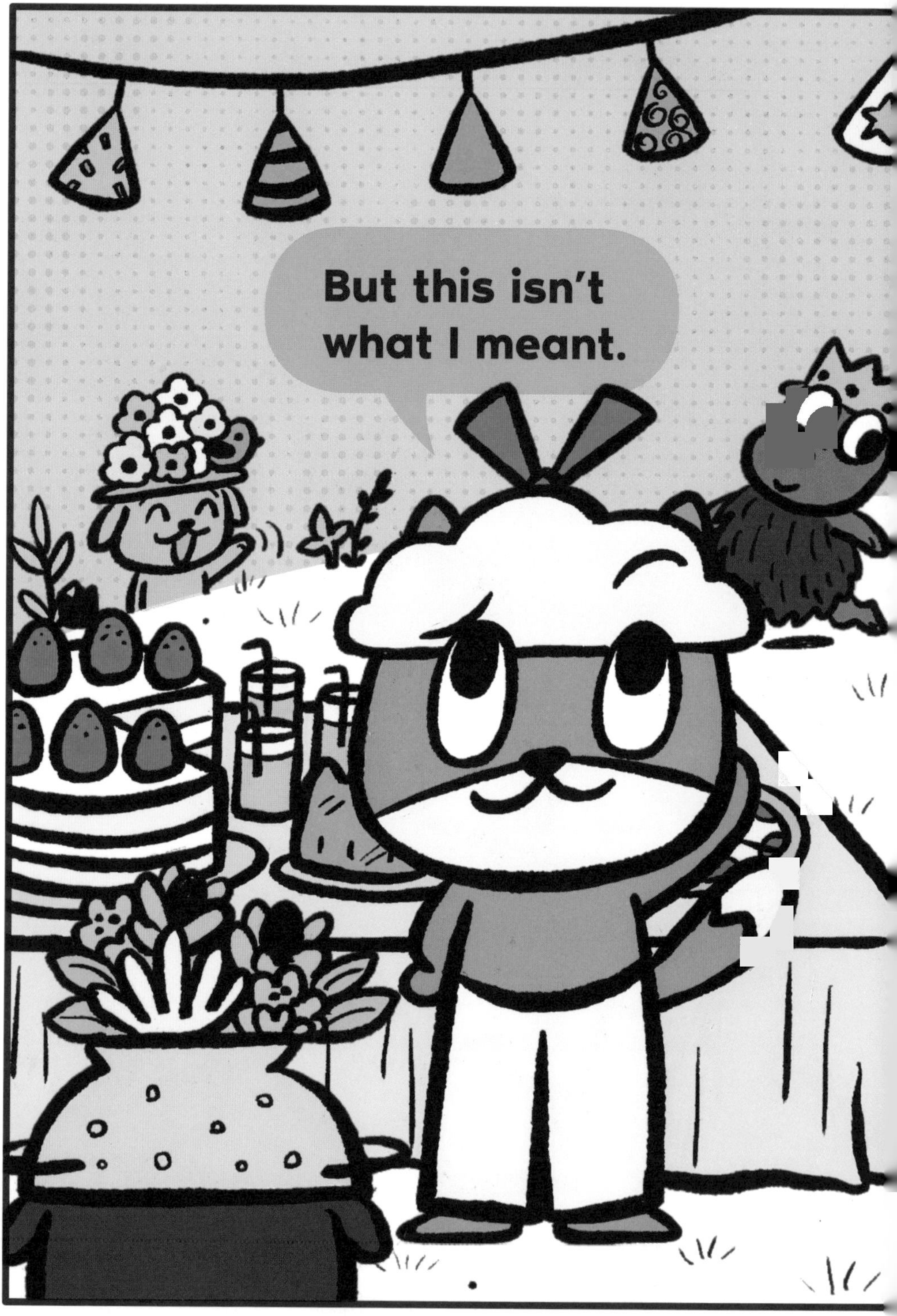
But this isn't what I meant.

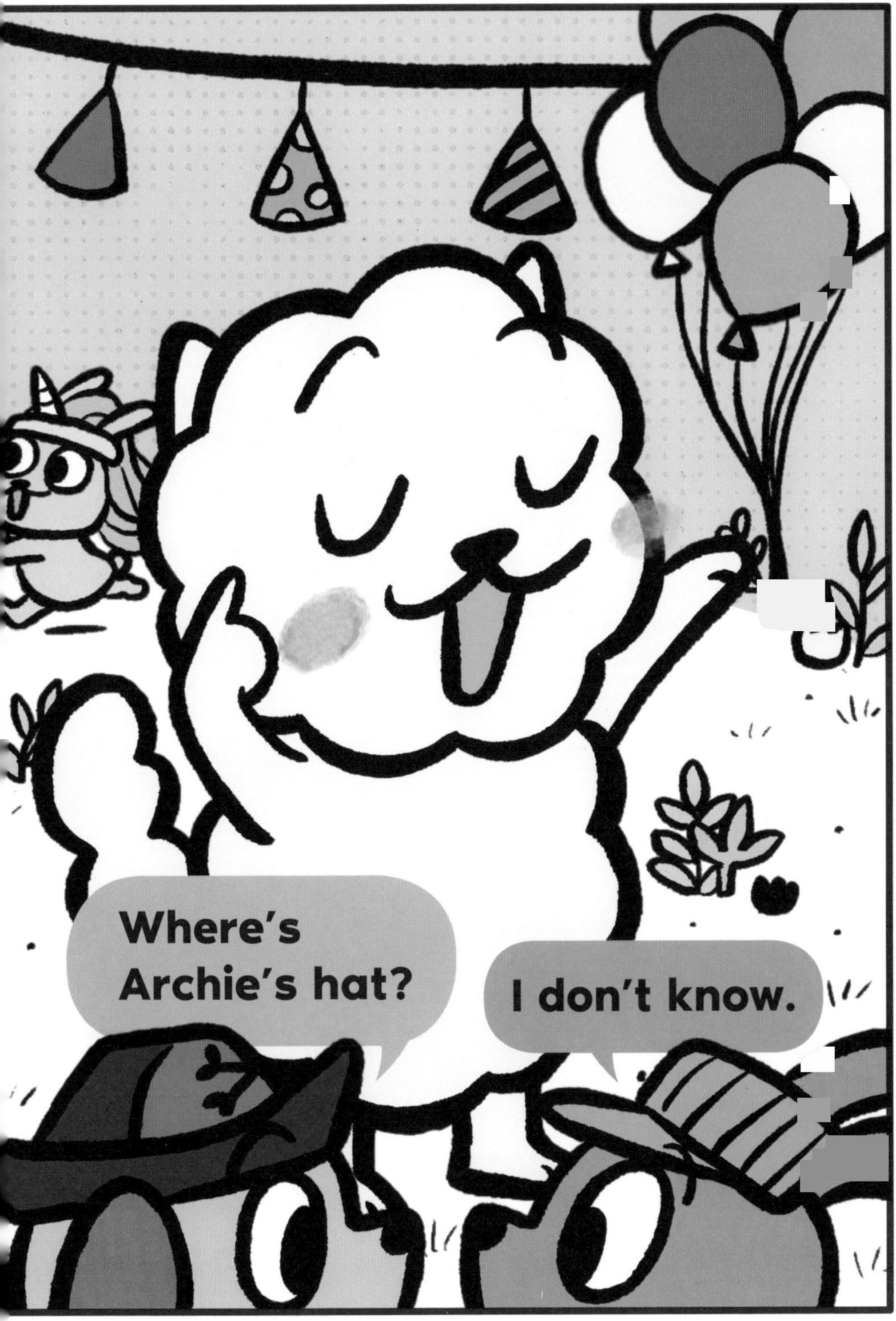
Where's Archie's hat?
I don't know.

MEET THE MAKERS

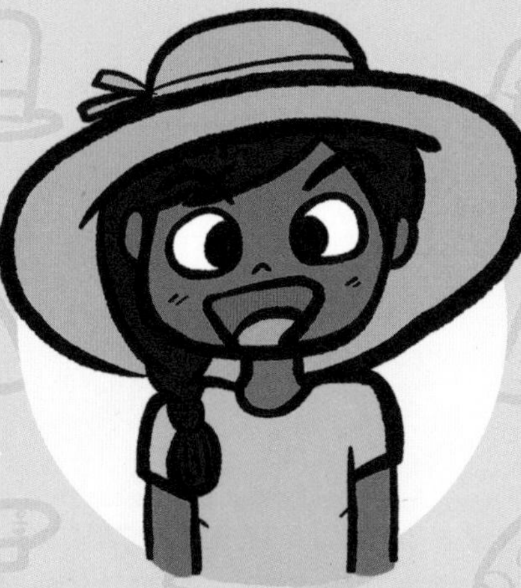

CANDY
draws

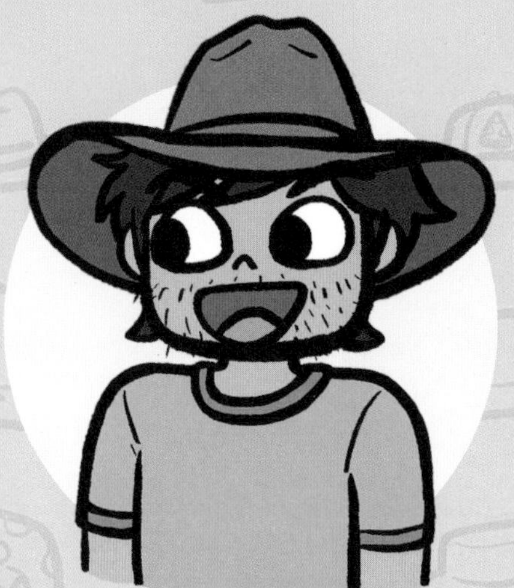

JAMES
writes

Candy James is a husband-and-wife creative duo originally from Hong Kong and New Zealand, but now living on a thickly forested hill in Ballarat, Australia. They are toy, graphic, and garden designers who love to make funny books for children.

What's their favorite hat?

Big floppy hats to keep the fierce Australian sun off their faces!

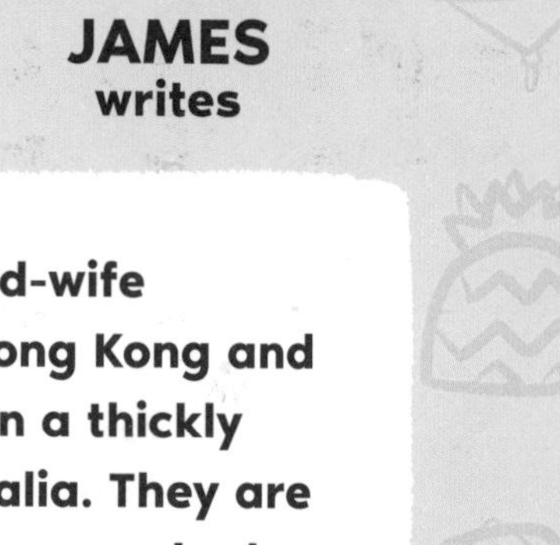

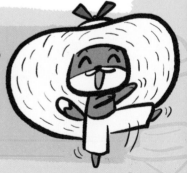